V25 (10-94) 3
Be
EEM-15
R34

LAST BOAT TO FORT BENTON

LAST BOAT TO FORT BENTON

•

JAMES A. JANKE

AVALON BOOKS
THOMAS BOUREGY AND COMPANY, INC.
401 LAFAYETTE STREET
NEW YORK, NEW YORK 10003

W

PRINTED IN THE UNITED STATES OF AMERICA
ON ACID-FREE PAPER
BY HADDON CRAFTSMEN, SCRANTON, PENNSYLVANIA

To Laura

Chapter One

The hungry flames chewed and clawed at the steamboat's planking and bulkheads, gobbling up the stacked cordwood and feasting on the bowels of the proud vessel. Her superstructure collapsed with a moan and screech of agony; an enormous cloud of sparks and smoke mushroomed upward into the dark sky.

"There she goes," Captain Zachary Cole sighed with a wince. He was leaning against a stanchion on the boiler deck of his own steamboat, the *West Wind*, half a mile away at the opposite end of the St. Joseph levee. He uncrossed his arms and blew into his cupped hands; the April nights were still cold in Missouri.

Burt Moore, Cole's first mate, sat on a railing next to him, leaning inboard with his elbows propped on his knees and trimming a thumbnail with a long-bladed knife. He looked back over his shoulder. "She was a good boat, too," he commented. He returned to his carving. "I say it could've been some die-hard Rebs, Zach."

"Maybe," Cole said. "More likely just some rooster down in the hold with a candle looking for whiskey. If I were going to torch a steamboat, I'd wait till there was a morning breeze and maybe get several boats at once."

Moore considered that. "You got a point." He glanced at the hint of yellow in the eastern sky. "And no breeze for awhile." He finished with the knife and slipped it back into its sheath. "And just how many more dawns are we goin' to watch just sittin' here in St. Joe, Zach?"

1

"The hold's still half empty, Burt," Cole told him. "Before going on upriver I want to replace the ninety tons of army supplies we delivered from St. Louis."

"We've been here over a week already," Moore complained. He dropped off the railing and turned to watch the conflagration in the distance. "There just ain't that much freight goin' north from St. Joe. And we already lost all our passengers 'cept one. The rest've transferred to other boats pushin' on. The *Mountain Queen*, the *Big Horn*, the *Pathfinder*, the—"

"I think Major Van Hill will stay as long as I keep the bar open," Cole said. "Besides, we're smaller and faster than those other boats. We may overtake them, anyway."

Moore shrugged. "Well, if we wait much longer we're gonna get stopped by low water way short of Fort Benton. And I don't relish freightin' our cargo overland halfway across Montana Territory."

"I know the risks," Cole said patiently. He realized that all his first mate saw was the great amount of work involved in navigating the Upper Missouri in low water. Moore was not considering the huge profits possible by reaching Fort Benton with a full cargo instead of one half empty.

Moore was quiet for awhile, watching the burning steamboat. "Maybe if we left now we could make two trips this summer," he said. "Steamboats've been gettin' all the way to Fort Benton only for the last five years. Nobody's tried two trips before. Light as we are we could probably make it up there in record time. Then race back to St. Louis, get another half load and—"

"And maybe lose the *West Wind* to low water in July," Cole said. "Too risky. We'll wait until—"

"Captain Cole?" a voice called from below.

Two men stood at the foot of the *West Wind's* landing stage. "Yes," Cole answered. "I'm Captain Cole. What can I do for you?"

"Is it too early in the morning to discuss business?"

Cole straightened up. "Certainly not, sir," he replied quickly. "Come aboard. My office is up here."

"Thank you, Captain." The man who had spoken walked briskly up the landing stage to the main deck, followed by the second man at a respectful distance.

Moore sidled closer to Cole. "The one in front looks pretty well-heeled, Zach," he whispered.

The two visitors ascended the forward stairs to the boiler deck, and Cole and Moore stepped over to meet them.

"Captain Zachary Cole at your service, gentlemen," Cole said shaking hands with the first man.

"Thaddius Kingsley, Captain," the man announced. "And this is my associate, Mr. Raasch."

"Mr. Raasch," Cole said. Raasch nodded slightly without offering a handshake. "And may I introduce my first mate, Mr. Moore," Cole continued. Kingsley shook Moore's hand.

Cole quickly sized up the two men. Kingsley was middle-aged, gray-haired, with an aspect of authority and self-importance about him. His clothes were clean and well tailored, though they seemed a bit baggy, as if the man had recently lost a lot of weight.

Raasch's appearance contrasted sharply with Kingsley's. Raasch was only slightly older than Cole and had a lean, muscular physique and a confident, almost belligerent manner of holding his big frame, with a penetrating stare that revealed nothing of his thoughts. His clothes were rough and looked like they'd been lived in for weeks. Cole also noted a pistol tucked into his belt.

"My office is this way, Mr. Kingsley," Cole directed.

The group followed Cole to the forward cabin on the starboard side of the boiler deck superstructure. Inside the lighted compartment Cole pulled out a chair for Kingsley and sat down at a desk himself. Moore took up a position against an inner bulkhead, while Raasch lounged against the cabin's outer doorjamb.

"Some excitement down at the other end of the levee this morning," Cole began idly.

"Captain," Kingsley said, "I would like to dispense with the amenities and get right down to business."

Cole nodded. "By all means, sir."

"I have a shipment for Fort Benton in Montana Territory," Kingsley stated. "I believe you are about to depart for that destination yourself."

Cole nodded again. "That's correct, sir. How much freight do you have?"

"I'd say slightly under a hundred tons."

Cole spread his hands in delight. "That's splendid, splendid," he said. "It just so happens I have half my cargo space available."

"That, too, was my information. What are your rates?"

"From here to Fort Benton, ten cents a pound."

"That's competitive with other boats. It's about 2,000 miles to Fort Benton, isn't it?"

"And then some," Cole said.

"Very well," Kingsley said. "Now, 100 tons at ten cents a pound is . . . . "

"Twenty thousand dollars, sir," Cole said quickly.

Kingsley smiled. "You have a quick mind for figures, Captain."

It was Cole's turn to smile. "That's good business. And, Mr. Kingsley, I'm afraid I must insist on payment in advance."

"That, too, is only good business," Kingsley responded. "Very well, my freight will be here within the hour." He rose briskly.

Cole reached for a pen and paper on his desk. "Who is the shipment to be consigned to?" Cole asked.

"I will accompany the shipment, Captain," Kingsley said. "I will need three single cabins and deck passage for thirty."

Cole raised his eyebrows as Moore blurted, "Thirty? That's quite a crew."

"I take it then, Mr. Kingsley, that your cargo is not dry goods?" Cole ventured. "Mining equipment, perhaps?"

"Exactly, sir."

"Ah," Cole said with a smile of understanding. "You don't intend to sell to the miners; you are going to dig the gold up yourself. And no placer mining for you, eh?"

"Precisely, sir," Kingsley said.

"Well, I caution you about hiring some of the men you'll find unoccupied in this town right now. The war soon ending has set some pretty desperate men adrift—"

Kingsley interrupted. "I am in a hurry, Captain," he said. "But I will choose carefully."

Cole rose. "Well, I believe you have the right idea. There's been little work done in the Montana goldfields so far. The war has held up any exploration since gold was discovered there a couple of years ago. But this spring Grant's going to bust Lee's line at Petersburg and take Richmond soon as the roads dry out. Then there'll be a rush out here that—"

"Really, Captain, I'm a very busy man. How much is the passenger fare?"

Cole didn't care for Kingsley's curtness, but it didn't matter. "Cabin passage to Fort Benton is 100 dollars a person. Deck passage is fifty."

"That makes a total of 1,800 dollars for the passengers," Kingsley said.

"That's correct, sir," Cole agreed.

"Very well," Kingsley said. He shook hands with Cole again. "Good day then, sir. I shall return shortly."

"It's a pleasure doing business with you, Mr. Kingsley," Cole said with a genuine smile on his face.

Kingsley strode out the door and Raasch followed briskly. Cole and Moore went to the boiler deck railing and watched the two men descend the landing stage of the *West Wind* and head up the levee, cutting a swath through the growing crowd that had come to gawk at the burning steamboat or to start the day's work.

"You see, Burt, a little patience can pay off handsomely," Cole said. He was still smiling broadly.

"You're right, Zach," Moore admitted.

Cole glanced to the east; the sky had grown quite bright. "Well, get the roosters up," he said. "There'll be plenty of work for 'em in an hour. See that they get a good breakfast."

"Aye aye, sir."

Chapter Two

Exactly one hour after he'd left the *West Wind*, Thaddius Kingsley returned in a hired carriage, leading a train of heavy freight wagons. They threaded their way through the bustle of teamsters on the levee and the crowds still staring at the blackened remains of the burnt steamboat.

Cole and Moore were waiting at the head of the *West Wind's* landing stage. They watched Kingsley get out of the carriage and head toward them, followed closely by another man carrying a large satchel and a big pistol strapped conspicuously to his waist. Raasch was busy giving orders to men and directing the wagons.

Kingsley strode up the landing stage and stopped in front of Cole and Moore. He motioned toward the man with him. "This is Peter Devlin, gentlemen, one of my employees." Devlin was tall and thin, with taut muscles and an alert bearing. His young face seemed prematurely aged. He touched his hat, and Cole nodded an acknowledgment. Kingsley said, "I hope you are ready to start loading, Captain. Mr. Raasch and my men will assist."

"Yes, sir," Cole answered. "As long as you have the charges with you." He glanced at the satchel.

"It's all here," Kingsley said.

Cole smiled and motioned with a hand. "Let's go to my office. Mr. Moore, start the loading."

"Aye aye, sir," Moore responded.

"The first two wagons are coming with me," Kingsley told him. "All the rest are merely carrying freight."

Cole looked pained. "I wish you had informed me earlier about the wagons, Mr. Kingsley. We made no arrangements for carrying teams. We'll have to take some time to build corrals and get feed for them. And of course there will be a considerable extra charge."

"I'm not taking the teams, Captain," Kingsley said. "Just the wagons."

Cole raised an eyebrow. "Horses are pretty scarce up in Montana Territory, Mr. Kingsley."

"I'll take that risk, Captain. No horses."

"Very well, sir," Cole acknowledged. "Carry on, Mr. Moore."

"Aye aye, sir." Moore turned and faced the gang of roustabouts lounging on the deck. "All right, you roosters," he shouted. "You're going to earn your pay today. Move! Move!"

The roustabouts got to their feet and trudged down the landing stage, Moore at their heels.

Kingsley and Devlin followed the captain up the forward stairs to his office. Inside, Kingsley took the satchel from Devlin. He set it on the desk, opened it, and pulled out a handful of currency.

"I will count it in your presence, Captain," Kingsley said.

Cole nodded. He folded his hands behind his back and watched intently as the other man counted out stacks of twenty- and fifty-dollar banknotes.

"Hard to find large-denomination bills these days," Kingsley observed. "This may take awhile." He looked at Devlin. "You count the coins, Devlin."

"Yes, sir," the other man said. He reached into the satchel and scooped up handfuls of coins, dumping them onto the desktop. The gold coins clattered and jingled, and some ran in little circles before finally wobbling to rest. Devlin started stacking the coins in piles of 100 dollars each.

Cole watched the piles and stacks grow, delighted in the

twinkle of sunlight on the gold coins and the pleasant musty smell of bills that had changed hands many times. He paid scant attention to the noises from outside, the creaking of wagon wheels on the landing stage, Moore's barked orders, Raasch shouting, boxes clunking, the tread of many boots.

But Moore interrupted Cole's concentration. "Captain Cole."

"What is it, Mr. Moore?" Cole asked. He didn't look up.

"Sir, I'd like you to take a look at something out here."

Both Kingsley and Devlin stopped their counting and looked at Moore.

"I'll be there shortly, Mr. Moore," Cole said.

"Sir, I wish you'd take a look right now," Moore insisted. "It's important."

Cole sighed. "Oh, all right," he said. "Mr. Kingsley, you must excuse me, sir."

"Of course, Captain," Kingsley responded.

Cole strode quickly after Moore. "It had better be important, Burt," he muttered.

Moore went to the railing overlooking the forecastle deck. "Zach, look down there. Take a gander at Kingsley's men."

Cole scrutinized Moore's face for a moment and was puzzled at the uneasiness he saw there. He looked down.

His gaze went from one man to the next, carefully noting each man's manners, his clothes, his build, his attitude. Cole frowned. "Hm, I see what you mean, Burt."

"Zach, that's no thirty men scraped up from the gutters and wharfs of St. Joe," Moore declared. "They're lean, mean, tough, and weathered. They work like dogs and obey orders—" He snapped his fingers. "—like that. Zach, there ain't one of those men that ain't straight outa the Reb army."

Cole's eyes continued to dart about.

"And," Moore added, quietly but emphatically, "they're all armed to the teeth, too."

"Nobody would go to Montana without weapons, Burt," Cole pointed out idly.

"Zach, I think they're mercenaries. I'll bet they had a hand in that fire this morning. And maybe they got their eye on the *West Wind*."

Cole drummed his fingers on the railing and was silent a moment. "They don't look like mercenaries, Burt. Too disciplined. They act like they're used to working together. All from the same outfit." Cole looked at Moore. "Kingsley's outfit? Now, Kingsley sure doesn't look like a mercenary. I know the countryside's swarming with Confederate deserters, Burt, and that the scum of 'em have formed some pretty bloodthirsty bands, but these men—"

"You've heard what happens when mercenaries get hold of a steamboat, Zach," warned Moore. "Stealin', burnin', killin' . . ."

Cole nodded vigorously. "Yes, yes, I know." He turned to face Moore. "But it doesn't make sense, Burt." He swept a hand toward the line of wagons. "Why would Kingsley bother to bring all that mining equipment with him if he simply wanted to torch this boat?"

"Maybe it ain't mining equipment," Moore suggested.

Cole considered that. "Well, let's take a look."

He led the way down the forward stairs to the forecastle deck and walked toward the landing stage. He stopped a man carrying a heavy wrought-iron cylinder. "Hold it," he said. "I want to look in that."

The man put the cylinder down, then took a deep breath and let it out slowly. "Sure is heavy for such a small thing," he declared.

Cole unscrewed the cylinder's metal lid and peered inside, then rocked the cylinder back and forth until a silvery liquid splashed out and formed little shiny puddles on the planking. He stabbed at the glistening beads with his finger, feeling the heavy liquid metal. "Mercury," he said. "For leaching gold from ore."

Cole stood up and handed the screw top back to the man. "Okay," he said. The man nodded and bent down to screw the lid back on.

Cole walked off the boat and up to the nearest wagon. He and Moore watched men struggle to remove the heavy contents of the wagon. Cole inspected the contents of several of the boxes and crates.

"What's been loaded already, Burt?" Cole asked.

"Lumber, timbers, kegs of nails, tools, and those two wagons with their loads."

Cole looked back at the cargo being stowed on deck and at what still remained on the wagons. "Burt, it sure looks like mining equipment to me. Still . . . "

"You want me to go get the provost marshal?" Moore asked. "I saw one of his patrols down near that burnt steamboat."

Cole frowned, considering the situation.

"Captain Cole," Kingsley said from behind the two men.

Startled, Cole spun around. "Yes, Mr. Kingsley?"

Kingsley, his hands behind his back, lowered his head a bit, eyes peering from under his brow. "A word with you, sir. In private."

Cole stared at the man, unsure of him. "All right," he said finally. He followed Kingsley a few paces off to the side.

Kingsley stopped and faced Cole. "Captain Cole," Kingsley began slowly. "I overheard what you and Mr. Moore were discussing."

Cole stiffened and folded his arms across his chest. "And?" he asked. His eyes wandered, seeking a glimpse of that blue-coated patrol Moore had mentioned.

"I throw myself—and my men—on your mercy, Captain Cole," Kingsley said.

Cole's arms slumped to his sides. "I don't understand."

"Suppose, sir," Kingsley said, raising a finger, "that there was a gentleman of considerable means whose devotion to the Confederate cause led him to raise a regiment in his county all at his own expense.''

''I've heard of that,'' Cole said.

''Well, sir, the South has been devastated by the war. This gentleman and his men have all been ruined by the war, their farms destroyed, their slaves freed, their stock run off or eaten by ravaging Yankees. What do you suppose these men should do, now that the war is ending? Go back to their ruined lands? To their starving families?''

''Seems reasonable to me,'' Cole said.

Kingsley slowly shook his head. ''Don't you suppose that these men, after spending years at war, would rather spend a few more months and the last of their colonel's fortune working hard to ensure that they go back to their families with enough to start over again?''

''You mean filling their pockets with Montana gold?''

Kingsley nodded.

Cole frowned. ''But why does this gentleman need secrecy?'' he began. ''He and his men need only turn themselves in to the nearest Federal military authority, swear not to fight any more, sign a parole, and be on their way again. It happens a lot nowadays.''

''Ah, but not always, Captain,'' Kingsley pointed out. ''Suppose, instead of parole, they are sent off to some military prison, if only for the summer. Then they would go back to their families empty-handed, with winter coming and no crops, no harvest, and no money. So surrendering is risky.''

Cole was silent. Was this a trick to get aboard the *West Wind* in order to burn her? But why a hundred tons of freight? And all that cash? Why not simply jump the *West Wind* at some yard or landing?

He could play it safe and refuse Kingsley passage. But if he did that the stacks of gold coins and greenbacks sitting on his desk would disappear. Over 20,000 dollars. And then some other steamboat captain might get them.

"Father," a distant female voice called out.

Kingsley looked past Cole and a smile spread on his face.

Turning, Cole saw a young woman approaching them. The breeze now blowing along the levee touched the wide brim of her hat and fluffed out long curly tresses of chestnut hair that cascaded down her shoulders, framing large brown eyes and attractive red lips. Layers of clothing could not conceal a figure that stopped all work on either side of the young woman as the workmen's eyes followed her progress toward Kingsley and Cole.

She clamped a hand down on her flapping hat as she stopped in front of the two men. "Hello, father," she said. She reached up and gave him a peck on the cheek. Then she looked at Cole. "Hello. You must be Captain Cole," she said, smiling sweetly.

"Captain Cole, my daughter, Rebecca," Kingsley said.

"How do you do, Miss Kingsley?" Cole said brightly. He bowed slightly and touched the bill of his cap. He hoped his captain's tunic did not look dishevelled. Then he noticed the carriage she had arrived in turning down a side street. He jerked his head back to look at Kingsley. "Is she one of the cabin passengers?" he blurted.

Kingsley bristled. "Certainly you don't expect her to travel on deck, do you?" he snapped.

"No, no, my apologies, sir," Cole said quickly. "I meant was she going on the trip with us? You made no mention of a lady passenger."

"An oversight on my part, Captain. Is there is some difficulty with that?"

A smile grew on Cole's face. The man was taking his daughter with him! "No, sir. Absolutely not." He smiled at Rebecca. "Delighted to have you on the trip, Miss Kingsley."

"Thank you, Captain Cole."

"Well, Captain," Kingsley asked slowly, "does that mean our transaction will proceed?"

Cole smiled. "Go back aboard, Mr. Kingsley," he said. "I'll be up directly."

"Thank you, sir." He offered an arm to Rebecca. "Come along, daughter."

"Yes, father," she said. Looking back at Cole, she added, "A pleasure to meet you, Captain."

"The pleasure was all mine, Miss Kingsley," Cole said eagerly.

Cole watched the couple head toward the *West Wind's* landing stage.

"That is one fine lookin' woman," Moore said. He had stepped up next to Cole unnoticed.

"And she sets my mind at ease, Burt," Cole said. "Kingsley wouldn't bring his daughter along if there was any chance of a gunfight. He really is headed for the goldfields."

"And I hope it's a slow trip," Moore said, still watching Rebecca as she disappeared into Cole's office.

"Yes indeed," Cole seconded. "Have all the luggage brought up to the appropriate cabins."

"Aye aye, sir." Moore hurried away.

Cole walked up the landing stage to the main deck and headed for the boilers. The steamboat's three boilers were located on the forward part of the main deck, underneath the boiler deck above, and with the firebox doors facing forward. Fresh air was sucked in at that point, and the heated air passed down the length of the three horizontal cylinders and back again before exiting up through tall smokestacks that pierced both boiler and hurricane decks above. Cole found Sam O'Brien directing a fire gang stuffing four-foot lengths of logs into the firebox.

"How's our steam, Mr. O'Brien?" Cole asked.

"Up to seventy pounds now, sir," the engineer informed him. "Gimme half an hour and we'll have twice that."

"Good," Cole commented. "Let me know when we hit one hundred and twenty."

"Aye aye, sir."

Cole took the forward stairs two at a time and found the Kingsleys and Devlin waiting for him in his office.

"We have the money all counted out, Captain Cole," Kingsley said.

"Fine, Mr. Kingsley," Cole answered. But he was looking at Rebecca. "Hope you have a ribbon to lash that hat down with, Miss Kingsley," he said. "You'll find the wind on the Upper Missouri rather strong. I've seen some winds in my day, but with all those open stretches of prairie around—"

"Your day, Captain?" the young woman scoffed gently. "Really now, you don't look much older than I am. In fact, I find it hard to believe you're old enough to be a steamboat captain."

Cole allowed himself a proud smile. "Been on the river for over fifteen years. Started as a decksweep. But the last few years have been quite rewarding. I've been captain and owner of the *West Wind* for eighteen months now." He hoped the brass buttons on his tunic were shiny enough.

"Oh, so the war has been profitable for you?" she asked, a smile on her face.

Cole's own smile evaporated slowly. Her voice and expression were congenial, but her words had a sharp edge to them.

"Rebecca, don't be rude," Kingsley interrupted. "Captain?" He waved a hand toward the money on the desk. "If you would please check this."

"Yes, of course," Cole said.

"Feel free to recount it, Captain," Kingsley offered. "That's only good business."

"No need," Cole said. "I can see you are a man of honor." He stepped over to a small closet in the far corner of the cabin and opened the door. Inside lay a large iron-strapped box. Cole fished in his vest pocket for a key. He opened the padlock on the strongbox and lifted the lid, then returned to the desk and transferred the gold coins and banknotes to the box. He lowered the lid and locked the box.

"I'll give you a receipt, sir," he said, slipping the key back into his vest pocket. He sat down at the desk and opened a drawer to reveal a Colt revolver plainly visible on top of assorted papers and ledgers.

"A handy place to keep a pistol, Captain," Kingsley commented.

"You never know when you might want one in a hurry," Cole replied.

"You actually have quite an arsenal in here," Kingsley noted. He was looking at the gun rack on the back bulkhead of the cabin. Half a dozen rifles and carbines were locked in place. They were mostly muzzle-loading Springfield muskets, but there was one breech-loading Sharps, and a lever-action Henry rifle as well.

"I see you have one of the new repeating Henrys," Kingsley observed.

"Worth more than all the rest put together," Cole agreed. He reached into the drawer and brought out a receipt book. With a pen freshly dipped into a desktop inkwell, he wrote out a receipt for Kingsley. "There you are, sir," he said. "And thank you."

Kingsley nodded. He folded the paper and stuck it into a pocket of his coat. "How soon before we leave?"

"Soon as the loading is finished and we have steam up. Shouldn't be long. In the meantime," he added, rising from his chair, "why don't you let me show you to your cabins."

"That will be fine, Captain," Kingsley said. "Devlin, report to Mr. Raasch."

"Yes, sir." Devlin left through the outside cabin door.

"This way, please," Cole said. He motioned to the inside cabin door, then stood aside to let the other people exit first.

"The *West Wind* may be small," he said as the couple entered the salon, "but we'll make you comfortable. Steamboats pride themselves on being the match of any hotel

cabin. He set the heavy burden down in a corner. "There you is, ma'am," he said.

"Thank you," Rebecca returned as Josh backed out through the door and left.

"Mr. Moore, is the loading completed yet?" Cole asked.

"Almost, sir," the first mate answered. "There's still some room in the hold, but some of them big crates'll have to ride on the deck. They're too big to get through the hatches."

"And the wagons?"

"Lashed down between the for'ard superstructure and the engine room aft."

"Very well. Has the decksweep come back yet?"

"No, sir."

"Hm. Wish he'd hurry. All right, Mr. Moore."

"Aye aye, sir." Moore touched the bill of his cap and smiled at Rebecca before he left.

"Perhaps you folks would like to get settled in your cabins," Cole suggested. "I'll be forward somewhere."

"I do have some things to take care of, Captain," Kingsley said.

"I'd just as soon watch the loading," Rebecca said. "May I join you, Captain?"

"By all means, Miss Kingsley," Cole said cheerfully. "I'd be delighted."

"Excuse me, then," Kingsley said. He left the cabin through the inside door as Cole and Rebecca walked up the promenade.

"Spent much time on steamboats, Miss Kingsley?" Cole inquired.

"Oh, yes," she said. "Our home is on the Mississippi. Tennessee. We've made quite a few trips to Vicksburg and New Orleans."

"Well, I'm afraid the *West Wind* can't match some of those floating palaces on the Mississippi, but I daresay you'll find steamboating on the Missouri, at least the Upper Missouri, quite different from that on the Mississippi in other ways as well.'' They had reached the forward railing of the boiler deck.

''Captain,'' O'Brien called from below. ''Steam's at a hundred and twenty.''

''Thank you, Mr. O'Brien,'' Cole acknowledged. ''Please attend to the main engines and leave Mr. Moore in charge of the fire gang.''

''Aye aye, sir.''

''Mr. Moore,'' Cole called. ''Any sign of Billy yet?''

''Yes, sir,'' Moore answered. He pointed down the levee. ''Here he comes now.''

''Good,'' Cole said. ''My decksweep,'' he said to Rebecca. ''Just twelve years old, but does a full day's work.'' He turned and watched the boy come bounding up the landing stage carrying a large sack in front of him. ''How'd you make out, Billy?'' Cole called.

The decksweep lowered the sack to the deck. ''Look at my shirt, Captain,'' he complained. ''It's practically shredded.''

Cole laughed. ''I'll get you a new one in Fort Benton.''

''Where do you want 'em, Captain?'' the lad asked.

''Down the forward hatch with 'em, Billy,'' Cole directed.

Billy began fiddling with a cord tied around the neck of the sack.

''What's in the sack, Captain Cole?'' Rebecca asked.

''Cats,'' Cole told her.

''Cats?'' she repeated in surprise.

''Uh-huh.'' Billy shook the sack over the open forward hatch, and four hissing, screeching cats fell into the dark hold. ''Steamboats are overrun with mice and rats, Miss Kingsley,'' Cole informed her, ''but the stores and settlements in Montana are much worse. Cats are a matter of survival up there. So, pound for pound, cats are about my most valuable cargo.''

"Fancy that," Rebecca said.

Moore was shouting below. "All right, bring in the landing stage! Get that hatch cover on. Okay, lay into it! Heave! Heave!"

Roustabouts manhandled the forward hatch cover into place. Block and tackle squeaked and rattled as the heavy landing stage was raised and brought aboard.

"Well, your father will be glad to learn that we can leave now, Miss Kingsley," Cole said.

"Fine. Who's your pilot?"

"Mr. Robert Kellogg will be on duty first."

"Is he good?" she asked.

"He's the second best pilot on the Upper Missouri," Cole declared.

"Second best?" Rebecca asked. "Who's the first best?"

"I am," Cole stated. He didn't smile.

But Rebecca did. "I should have known."

"If you will excuse me now, Miss Kingsley, I must see to the departure." He touched the bill of his cap.

"Until later, Captain," she said, smiling pleasantly.

Cole was reluctant to leave Rebecca's company. He ascended the stairs to the hurricane deck and he crossed its short width before hopping onto the low skylight roof. At the window of the wheelhouse he stopped to talk with Kellogg.

"All set, Bob?" Cole asked.

"All set, Zach," Kellogg declared.

"Wait for my signal." Cole walked forward between the two immense black smokestacks and stepped to the very edge of the railingless deck and peered down onto the forecastle below. He noted the landing stage properly secured and Moore waiting with several roustabouts.

"Let go hawser, Mr. Moore," Cole called down.

"Aye aye, sir." Moore ordered two roustabouts to throw off the heavy line from the bitt at the bow.

"All clear, Captain," Moore said.

Cole turned to the wheelhouse. "All gone, Mr. Kellogg," he called. "Take her out."

Kellogg saluted and yanked on the cord that rang the signal bell in the engine room. Then he reached up and gave a long pull on the cord to the steam whistle. It blasted out a shrill, throaty scream that drifted down the levee and out over the city. Cheers broke out along the shore; it was a reflex action in any river town.

The *West Wind's* engines labored, puffing and chugging loudly. Slowly at first, then faster, the wide buckets of the steamboat's sternwheel flailed the muddy water, churned the surface, and sent froth and foam bubbling away from the boat. The *West Wind* backed slowly away from the levee.

Cole had always enjoyed departures. There was a sense of excitement, a promise of new experiences, and a feeling of adventure in leaving. But now that he had his own boat, he enjoyed the event even more. He liked to stand conspicuously on the hurricane deck, hands behind his back, an impassive expression on his face. He feigned boredom and disinterest when in reality he was proud and exhilarated, looking down from his lofty vantage point on the crowd that had turned to watch. The *West Wind* was his, all his.

Kellogg backed the steamboat out into the channel and swung her about until her bows pointed upstream. There was a short respite from the engines' pounding while the sternwheel was reversed. Then the chugging returned, brown water at the stern foamed and boiled, a bow wave appeared forward, and the *West Wind* forced herself upstream against the powerful current of the Missouri.

Cole remained at the forward edge of the hurricane deck. He enjoyed the sensation of standing high above the surface of the water, smelling the dampness of the river, sensing the mighty current, and feeling the breeze blow fresh and clean in his face.

He listened with his ears and his feet. The engines pounded with the powerful head of steam pressure driving them; the boilers were at peak performance, not yet clogged with sediment from the muddy river water used in them.

"Captain Cole," Major Van Hill said behind him.

Cole flinched. Lost in his reverie, he had not heard Van Hill approaching. "What is it, Major?" Cole asked. Then he noticed the look on the officer's face. "Something wrong?" he said quickly.

"Captain Cole," Van Hill said urgently, "the boat is swarming with Rebels!"

"Oh," Cole said with relief. "You mean Kingsley's men."

Van Hill looked astonished. "You mean you knew they were Rebels and you let them aboard anyway?" he sputtered.

"They aren't Rebels anymore, Major," Cole said. "And they aren't a loose bunch of murderous rabble, either. Kingsley seems in pretty tight control of his men, army or no army, war or no war."

"The war's not over yet," maintained the major.

"It is for Kingsley and his men. They're headed for Montana while the gold pickings are still good. They've brought along enough equipment for a small mining operation and stamp mill. His men will have a profitable summer, and I'll bet Kingsley will get rich, if he stays up there."

"Once a Rebel, always a Rebel, Cole."

"Major, would Kingsley bring his daughter along if he meant to start a fight?"

Van Hill pondered the point. "A man like Kingsley doesn't abandon his cause just because it's lost," he said at last.

"Major, Kingsley's out to make some money for himself and his men, and I intend to get my share, too."

"Hmph," the Army officer snorted. "Long as a man's willing to pay, you don't ask questions, do you?"

"I'd say we're all going to have to stop asking questions,

Major,'' Cole snapped back. "Let the Union recover, start over again.''

"It'll be interesting to see if you still feel that way when Kingsley sends the *West Wind* up in flames around your ears.''

"I'll shoot him if he tries that,'' Cole said. Then he shook his head slowly. "But he doesn't want to burn the boat; he wants to go to Montana on it.''

Cole put a hand on Van Hill's shoulder. "Major, I appreciate your concern. I know that mercenaries make a particular point of killing any Union officers they find aboard steamboats. If you wish, I can let you off at the next landing or town.''

Van Hill straightened up and brushed off Cole's hand. "I run from no Rebel, Captain.''

"I didn't mean it that way, Major,'' Cole said. "But relax,'' he encouraged. "Enjoy the trip. Nothing's going to happen, I promise you.''

"Bah,'' Van Hill said. He spun on his heels and stalked off toward the stairs.

Cole sighed. He turned and faced forward again, irritated with Van Hill. If the man was to be stationed at Fort Rice, it meant he was probably about the worst officer in the Union Army. Only the dregs of the officer corps got stuck out on the frontier while the war was on. Yet Van Hill was acting like he was Grant himself.

Cole shook his head and turned his attention back to the Missouri River. They had passed the row of steamboats at the levee and he looked back fondly at them. When he returned from Fort Benton his profits would enable him to buy a part of one of those boats or maybe even another whole boat. The thought brought a wide grin to his face.

Chapter Three

Rebecca pulled the shawl tightly around her shoulders as she stopped next to Cole, who stood at the front of the boiler deck, hands spread wide on the railing.

"Good afternoon, Miss Kingsley," Cole greeted. He smiled cheerfully.

"Good afternoon, Captain," she said, smiling herself. She shivered. "It's very chilly today."

"The wind makes it worse," Cole conceded.

Rebecca nodded toward some birds on the river. "Those ducks don't seem to mind the weather."

Ducks were everywhere on the river, forming vast rafts containing a dozen species. The birds paddled leisurely out of the way of the steamboat or took flight, their feet pattering the surface until they gained enough speed to become airborne.

"Must be thousands of them," she ventured.

"Heading north," Cole said. "Both Dakota and Montana Territories are great breeding grounds for waterfowl."

"Any chance of getting some duck to eat?" she asked. "I'm sure father would be willing to do the hunting himself."

"No need, Miss Kingsley," Cole said. "The *West Wind* has her own hunter who travels ahead of the boat, bagging game for us. Right now it'll be duck and goose. Later there'll be antelope, deer, buffalo, even elk."

"I look forward to all of it," Rebecca said. "But, Captain, the boat seems to be heading for shore. Are we stopping?''

"Yes, ma'am," Cole informed her. "We're putting in for wood. Nodaway Island woodlot."

"But we already stopped for wood once today."

"We have to stop at least twice a day. We go through about thirty cords of wood a day, and we can't carry that much at one time."

"I didn't realize that. Father will be distressed at the frequent stops."

"Sorry, nothing I can do about it," Cole said.

With the *West Wind's* sternwheel thrashing the water in reverse to soften the blow, the steamboat's bow crunched up against the bank of the heavily wooded island.

"Secure the boat!" Moore yelled below. "Landing stage out! Move!"

Two roustabouts hopped to the bank with the end of a heavy line and gave it several turns around the stump of a massive tree.

"Woodpile!" Moore shouted. "Let's go, let's go!"

The roustabouts trooped off the boat and headed for the rows of stacked cordwood. Moore headed for the owner coming to meet the boat.

"Hmph," Cole snorted, eyeing the stacks of wood. "If we keep getting only cottonwood, like this woodhawk has, we'll have to stop three times a day, Miss Kingsley. Cottonwood doesn't burn well. It's smoky and burns too fast. Can't get even a hundred pounds of steam if all we're burning is cottonwood. Need hardwood. Ash preferably."

Moore called from the shore. "Captain, the man wants three-fifty a cord."

"All right," Cole shouted. "Take fifteen cords."

"Is that expensive?" Rebecca asked.

Cole shrugged. "It'll sound cheap farther up the river. We'll be paying nine dollars a cord by the time we get to Fort Benton."

"Wood is scarce upriver?"

"Very. Not many trees north of the Platte River, except along the river bottoms. After Omaha we'll stop at every woodlot and take on all the wood we can carry. Not to mention cutting our own wood, if we have to, and scrounging driftwood from racks hung up on the bars."

"No trees?" Rebecca asked, stricken. She scanned the trees along the island's thickly wooded shore. "It's going to be depressing without trees. I love trees."

"It is beautiful," Cole said. He stepped back. "But you must excuse me, Miss Kingsley," he said. "I have to relieve Mr. Kellogg at the wheel."

"May I join you?" Rebecca asked.

"Please do," Cole said.

"Looks like there are more trees in the river than there are on the shore," Rebecca observed while looking through the front window of the *West Wind's* wheelhouse.

Cole smiled. He gave the big wheel a slight turn. "We're in the middle of the April rise right now. The spring rains and the melting of the snow on the northern plains and foothills puts a lot of water into the Missouri. The river picks up dead trees on every sandbar and shoots 'em all downriver. Not to mention the trees it picks up by constantly carving away at the banks."

"The Missouri is much muddier than the Mississippi," Rebecca noted.

"Big Muddy they call it," Cole said. "Too thick to swim in, too thin to farm," he added with a smile. He paused. "You've never seen the Missouri before?"

"No," Rebecca told him.

"Well, the Missouri's a lot shoalier than the Mississippi. Can't navigate the Upper Missouri at all except in spring and part of the summer. Boats go up the river on the April rise and back down again on the June one, when the high altitude snows on the Rockies melt. If you miss that June rise, your boat's stuck up the Missouri until the next year. If it survives the winter ice that is.''

"Speaking of shallow," Rebecca said, "it looks awfully shallow up ahead.''

"It is," Cole told her. "That's Squaw Point. A river crossing.''

"You mean a ford for wagons?''

"No, no." He chuckled. "The channel crosses from one side of the river to the other. It always throws up sandbars in the eddies as it gulps away at the banks on the other side.''

Rebecca peered close to the window. "How do you know where to steer amongst all those bars? Do you remember which way you went last time?''

"Yes, but that's of no use. The river's always digging a new channel. It's never the same on any two trips.''

Cole leaned over to the speaking tube. "Mr. O'Brien," he called. "I want soundings taken. Put a man on the bow.''

A man with a long pole took up a position on one side of the forecastle deck. Another man appeared on the hurricane deck and ran forward to take up a post from where he could relay messages from the sounding man to the pilot.

The sounding man thrust his pole into the water, glanced at the marking at the waterline, then quickly yanked the pole back out. He shouted to the man on the hurricane deck, who yelled the sounding to Cole.

"Five feet!''

Cole gave the wheel a good turn, and the boat swerved sharply.

"How did you decide which side of that bar to take, Captain?" Rebecca asked.

"Can't be sure which chute of the two is the deeper, Miss Kingsley," Cole said, "but the wind seems to be rippling the one on our larboard side more than the one on our starboard side. The more rippling, the deeper the water—usually.''

"I see.''

"Four and a half!'' came the cry from the sounding.

"Getting shoalier,'' Cole noted. The *West Wind* continued on. Cole rang the signal bell for half speed.

"Four feet large!''

"Four feet,'' Rebecca repeated uneasily. "Surely our draft must be more than that.''

"No,'' Cole informed her. "We aren't drawing more than three and a half feet.''

"Is that all?''

"Four feet scant!''

"Doesn't look good,'' Cole judged. He rang the signal bell to reverse engines. "Let's give the other chute a try.''

The sternwheel stopped turning, and the *West Wind* quickly lost headway and started drifting downstream. The wheel reversed, and the boat accelerated backwards.

"Aren't we going fast enough without doing that?'' Rebecca asked anxiously.

"Can't steer if you're just drifting with the current, Miss Kingsley.'' Cole was facing the stern, watching the progress of the boat. "If you'd like a real ride, wait until we come back downstream. We really race along then.''

Cole faced forward again and rang the signal bell. "Let's try the other chute!'' he called.

Again the *West Wind's* sternwheel stopped and reversed. The boat shuddered, fought the current, then forged ahead. Cole steered her sharply to the other side of the river.

"Five feet!''

"We may be in luck,'' Cole said hopefully.

"Four feet!''

"It's changing fast,'' Rebecca observed earnestly.

"Three and a half!''

Cole shouted into the speaking tube. "Give me all you got, Mr. O'Brien!''

The boat lurched as her bottom rubbed the mud. The *West Wind* sagged to a halt.

"We're aground," the young woman exclaimed, aghast.

Cole smiled patiently. He rang to stop the engines. "This will become quite routine, Miss Kingsley, I assure you."

"Routine?" Rebecca asked, a frown on her face. "You mean you actually plan to run aground again?"

"Over and over again," Cole told her.

"Doesn't that damage the boat?" Rebecca asked.

"No. Missouri steamboats are built to take repeated groundings. They have flexible hulls, very loose construction. Why, they'd collapse of their own weight if it weren't for the hog chains."

"But now what do we do, Captain?"

"We're going to do some sparring," Cole said. "Come watch." He motioned to the door of the wheelhouse and Rebecca preceded him as they walked forward on the hurricane deck.

"Mr. Moore," Cole called down to the first mate. "Commence sparring."

"Aye aye, sir," Moore responded, but he had already set the roustabouts to work.

Suspended from derricks, one on each side of the forecastle and rising higher than the hurricane deck, were two huge wooden spars with iron tips driven into their lower ends. Moore directed the derricks to be swiveled outboard, and the spars were lowered into the river bottom, their tops projecting forward at an angle.

Two roustabouts lifted off one of the forward hatch covers and jumped into the hold. They were followed by Sam O'Brien.

Lines ran through block and tackle from the top of the spars down to pulleys on the deck, then over to the two capstans on the forecastle deck.

"Start the auxiliary engines," Moore called.

Two small steam engines in the forward hold chugged

into life and blew steam into the air. The capstans turned, lines tightened, wood creaked and groaned. Slowly the bow of the steamboat was lifted out of the water, and the entire vessel was dragged forward as the lines wound around the capstans.

"Hold it!" Moore called. "Slacken lines!"

Tension was released on the capstans and the lines unwound. The bow of the *West Wind* sank back into the water, but the boat was now a short distance ahead of its previous position.

The spars were hoisted out of the water and set forward again. The entire procedure was repeated. Again, the *West Wind* was dragged a little farther over the sandbar.

"Rather clever, Captain Cole," Rebecca complimented. "Makes us look like a big grasshopper."

"Matter of fact, that's what some call it—grasshoppering," Cole told her. "Every boat in the Missouri River trade uses it."

Rebecca nodded and stared at the spars. "But it'll take hours to get over a bar this way. Father will be greatly distressed at the frequent delays."

Cole said, "It will be getting dark soon. Maybe a good meal will distract him."

"Well, Captain," Thaddius Kingsley said, transferring another piece of roast duck onto his plate, "if we must stay tied up at the shore at night like this, at least this is excellent duck."

"Thank you, Mr. Kingsley," Cole said from his place at the head of one of the long tables in the *West Wind's* salon. Cole enjoyed these meals with his passengers. He liked the company and enjoyed the sense of being in command, of owning the situation.

On his immediate left sat Kingsley, with Rebecca next to him. On Cole's right was Major Van Hill.

Cole paused to allow the waiter to refill his wine glass. "I'm as frustrated as you are about not traveling at night, but even with a good moon it's too difficult to see snags and bars in the Missouri. On the Mississippi it would be different."

"I understand, sir," Kingsley said. He poked a mouthful of duck into his mouth.

"A most excellent selection of wines, too, Captain," Van Hill said.

Cole nodded absently. He was studying Rebecca. Although her father and Van Hill seemed to be relishing the meal, Rebecca merely picked at the food. "Miss Kingsley, the boat's hunter would be hurt to see how little of his game you are eating."

"No appetite, my dear?" Kingsley asked.

"It's not that, father," the woman answered. "It's just that it doesn't seem right for us to be feasting like this while so much of the South is starving."

"Surely, Miss Kingsley," the captain said, "it can't be wrong to merely harvest the bounty of the land we find around us. Our not eating the duck will not allow someone else in the South to do so." He reached for his wine glass and took a sip.

"And did the boat's hunter shoot that wine for you, Captain?" she asked.

Cole chuckled self-consciously. "Well, no," he admitted.

"Rebecca," Kingsley said with a frown. He knew his daughter's moods well and had a foreboding of what was coming.

"No doubt, Captain," Rebecca went on, "that wine was purchased with money paid you by the United States government to help invade my state."

She was smiling, but Cole had no doubt this time about her hostility. "I consider shipping freight for the Army to be duty as well as business," he said carefully.

Rebecca stabbed a piece of baked potato with her fork and thrust it into her mouth. She began chewing methodically.

"It'll all be immaterial soon, anyway," Van Hill said. "The war's about over."

"I wouldn't be too sure of that," Kingsley said.

Cole glanced at Kingsley. "Surely you don't think Lee's dwindling army will be able to resist Grant's overwhelming strength."

Kingsley shrugged. "Richmond's been the goal of the Union Army for four years, and Grant may find the prize just as elusive this year. Besides, Richmond isn't the Confederacy."

"But, Mr. Kingsley," Cole said. "The South is devastated. Her economy is a shambles, her industry ruined, her land scorched. And think of all the dead already. What can the South have to gain by further resistance?"

"I only know that there are some in the Confederacy who feel that surrender is unthinkable, regardless of cost." He continued to carve his piece of duck.

"If the South will not surrender," Van Hill said, "she will be beaten into submission."

Cole wished Van Hill didn't sound so pompous.

"And it's obvious," Rebecca retorted, glaring at Van Hill, "that the North will stop at nothing to impose its will upon the South. Including killing women and children and—"

"Rebecca," Kingsley snapped, putting down his knife and fork.

"Miss Kingsley," Van Hill said testily, "I don't know what you're referring to specifically, but—"

"Major Van Hill," Kingsley nearly shouted. Everyone looked at him. "I think it best to change the subject."

Van Hill nodded formally. "Many pardons, sir." He grabbed one of the rolls from a basket in the center of the table and made a great show of tearing it in half. Silence fell all around.

Cole shifted his glance repeatedly between Rebecca and her father. "Well, I guess you're all glad to see the weather warm up."

"The sun did feel good, sir," Kingsley said.

"Why, a month from now," Cole said, "you'll be complaining about the heat."

Another long pause.

"Captain," Van Hill said, jumping into the awkward gap in the conversation. "I hear three of your roustabouts deserted today."

Cole didn't think that was the best choice of a new subject, but he answered nonetheless. "They didn't desert, they quit. At the last woodyard." He didn't go on to explain that all his cajoling couldn't make the men stay; they were afraid of Raasch.

"Hmph," Kingsley muttered. "Well, your three men are a good illustration of the surprises in store for the Yankees. When a slave is freed he becomes completely irresponsible and shiftless."

Rebecca fixed hard eyes on Cole. "A black requires direction and discipline to make him useful and earn his keep, Captain Cole," she said.

"Perhaps," Cole granted. "But then, out of the seven dollars a week I pay a rooster, an owner would've gotten six. Now, the man gets all seven."

"A dubious benefit, Captain," Rebecca stated. "Out of that money, each man must now buy everything that was formerly provided for him by his owner."

"He can still do it," Cole argued. "Only now he chooses what he spends his money on."

"It is not the same," Rebecca said acridly. "I would be surprised if there was a single man among your roustabouts who didn't spend all of his money on liquor and loose women as soon as he hit the shore."

"Well," Van Hill muttered, "at least they don't waste it." He chuckled to himself and reached for his wine glass.

Cole glared at Van Hill. He wished the major didn't drink so much.

Rebecca jumped to her feet. "You Yankee hypocrites," she spat out. Cole flinched. Van Hill peered over the edge of his wine glass.

"Rebecca," Kingsley hissed.

"Both of you," she declared, glaring first at Van Hill and then at Cole. "You shout freedom for the slaves in your holier-than-thou piety—"

"Now just a minute, Miss Kingsley," Cole said hastily. "I never—"

"—but then you wash your hands of any responsibility for the poor souls after they have their so-called freedom. But they're not free. You've only imposed upon them another form of slavery, an economic slavery, more subtle but harsher, and whose only goal is making more money for you."

"Miss Kingsley," Cole declared, "I pay my men a fair wage."

Rebecca was breathing rapidly, her eyes glaring, her hand twisting her napkin into knots. She pointed accusingly at Van Hill. "You make me sick, Major. You invade our country, kill our men who try to defend their homes and their families. You murder defenseless women and—"

"Rebecca!" Kingsley exclaimed, leaping up from his chair. He grabbed his daughter by both shoulders and gave her a firm but gentle shake.

Rebecca stared angrily into his face for a moment. Then her features softened, her eyelids fluttered, and tears appeared at the corners of her eyes. "Oh, father," she moaned. Her head sank to his chest and he put his arms around her.

Kingsley patted his daughter on the shoulder. "Perhaps, dear, you would like to get some fresh air," he said.

She shook her head slightly as she raised it. "No, but I think I will go to my cabin."

"All right," Kingsley said.

Chairs scraped as Cole and Van Hill rose together.

Rebecca sniffled and dabbed at her eyes with the back of her hands. "Excuse me, gentlemen."

Cole and Van Hill nodded and mumbled reassurances.

Rebecca walked slowly toward her cabin. A moment later they heard the cabin door shut quietly behind her.

There was a long, awkward silence as the men, still standing, eyed each other. Finally Cole turned to the bar. "Cigars," he ordered. He sat down, and the others followed his lead.

The bartender arrived with an open humidor. Cigars were extracted, but still there was silence. It was not until curls of cigar smoke began wafting upwards that the silence was broken. Kingsley spoke.

"The women of the South will be the last to admit defeat, gentlemen," he said. "You must excuse my daughter."

"It was my fault," Cole stated. "It is my duty to prevent such confrontations."

Kingsley sighed. "The death of her mother was quite hard on her."

"I'm sorry," Cole said. "Recently?"

"Two years ago, but it was under circumstances that lent a certain timelessness to the event."

"How so?"

"Rebecca found her mother on the floor of our kitchen after a Federal shell had exploded in the room."

Cole winced. "I am truly sorry," he said. "That must have been incredibly hard on both of you."

"My loss was great, but the impact was less immediate for me. I was away at the time."

"I see."

Van Hill spoke, more softly than he had before. "Civilian

casualties are the most tragic of all war casualties. A stray shell—''

Kingsley cut him off. ''There was nothing stray about it, sir!'' he said angrily.

Cole frowned. ''I find that hard to believe.''

''Yankee gunboats on the Mississippi had been fired on by Confederate soldiers defending their homeland. The brave men made good their escape, so in frustration the gunboats retaliated by firing on the nearest buildings—my farm, my home, and,'' he concluded grimly, glaring at Van Hill, ''my wife.''

Van Hill said nothing, only stared back at Kingsley.

Cole said, ''I'm deeply sorry, sir.'' He sighed. ''There have been many deaths of innocents. And, yes, too many soldiers have died, too. Thank God there'll soon be an end to all the killing.''

Kingsley took an angry puff on the cigar in his hand. ''Some will always keep on fighting.''

Cole felt uneasy.

''But no dying to the last man for you, eh, Kingsley?'' Van Hill asked. ''Off to the goldfields!''

Kingsley's jaw tightened. He took the cigar out of his mouth and wagged it at Van Hill. ''I know of only one Nathan Van Hill,'' Kingsley growled. ''Only it was Colonel Van Hill then. At Chickamauga on the right of the Union line.''

Van Hill froze in his chair.

Cole noticed that the major's hand trembled as it reached for the cigar in his own mouth. His face had turned ashen.

''The right of the Union line collapsed. A regiment broke. Your regiment,'' Kingsley accused.

''I tried to stop them,'' Van Hill mumbled weakly. He dropped his cigar, ignoring the puff of ash as it hit the table.

''The story I heard,'' Kingsley insisted, ''was that you led the retreat. They only followed your dust.''

Van Hill pushed his chair back slowly and rose. Wordlessly he shuffled to the bar and motioned to the barman to bring him a bottle.

Kingsley turned to Cole. "I, on the other hand," he said firmly, "am not a coward." With that he rose and swaggered toward his cabin.

Cole watched Kingsley enter his cabin and close the door behind him. He noted with chagrin that now all of his guests had left him, and unhappily so.

Cole rose and walked cautiously up to the major.

Van Hill was pouring himself another drink at the bar, spilling some of the liquor onto the countertop. He tossed his head back and downed the entire contents of the glass. He set the glass down gently on the bar.

"It'll haunt me the rest of my life," Van Hill said. "A moment of indecision, a flitting wave of panic, a sudden loss of confidence. The Rebs were hitting us so hard. I took a few steps back and then suddenly we were all heading for the rear as fast as we could, each man's panic feeding that of the man next to him."

"General Thomas stood his ground, though," Cole said. "We all read about it. He stopped the Confederates. They managed to bottle you up in Chattanooga, but you got out of that eventually."

Van Hill poured himself another drink. "But I lost my command, Captain. That was two years ago. And I've been desperate to get another command ever since. Finally they sent me out here. I wish they'd shot me instead."

Now Cole understood why Van Hill was going to Fort Rice. "Life on the frontier can't be so bad," he said.

Van Hill looked at him in amazement. "But how will I win my name back, Captain?" he said. "The Sioux are some of the fiercest warriors on earth. And what does the Army have out here? Scum! The most worthless, drunken collection of misfits and criminals Washington could assemble in one place."

"For that matter," Cole said, "the Sioux seem pretty

quiet since they got so badly punished for their raids in Minnesota in '62. There may be no fighting at all.''

Van Hill drank down his liquor in one gulp. ''Captain, I'm heading for an oblivion called Fort Rice.'' Now he merely put the bottle to his lips, gulping at the brown liquid. Finally he lowered the bottle and wiped his mouth with the back of his hand.

Still holding the bottle in his hand, Van Hill wagged a finger at Cole. ''But I'll tell you one thing, sir,'' he declared. ''I'll never run from a Rebel again. I'll die first.''

Van Hill motioned for a second bottle, and the bartender gave it to him. ''I'm going to my cabin,'' he said to Cole. Then he shuffled off, a bottle in each hand. His cabin door closed quietly behind him.

Chapter Four

"Not more sparring, Captain," Kingsley complained, reaching Cole at the forward railing of the boiler deck. The *West Wind* was still moving, but she was rubbing bottom. Moore was already directing roustabouts at the derricks.

"Bethlehem Bar," Cole informed him. Kingsley laid his hands on the railing and sighed. "And it gets worse the farther up we go, Mr. Kingsley."

Kingsley nodded in resignation. Then he added, "I see there's another steamboat in the same predicament." He was looking at another vessel some distance ahead at the other end of the bar.

"All the boats have the same trouble here," Cole said.

Kingsley frowned. The crew of the other steamboat was loading cargo from the shore into yawls and transferring it to their steamboat. "Where'd that freight come from?" he asked. "This seems like an unlikely spot for a landing."

"It's not a landing, Mr. Kingsley," Cole told him. "That's cargo they already had aboard. We can manage to get over the bar with just sparring once, but that boat's so big, they had to resort to double-tripping."

"What's that?"

"Cargo is taken off a boat until she's light enough to be sparred over a bar. The boat goes upstream, unloads more of her cargo, then comes back down to pick up the first offloaded cargo and goes over the bar again. After picking up the second cargo they're back on their way."

41

Kingsley looked appalled. "I hope we don't have to double-trip."

Cole shook his head. "The *West Wind's* not that big."

"Good. How soon before we're over this bar?"

Cole looked over at the long shadows cast by the *West Wind* on the muddy water. "We might be over by dark."

"Hmph. And then another night wasted at the shore." The *West Wind* sagged to a halt and Kingsley shook his head in disgust. "Here we go again," he muttered.

Moore quickly had the two spars in place, and the auxiliary steam engines in the forward hold began their huffing and noisy chugging.

Rebecca strolled up to Cole and her father. "Captain Cole," she said stiffly.

Cole bowed slightly. "Good afternoon, Miss Kingsley," he said. He tried to be as pleasant as possible; he wished her attitude toward him had not soured.

"There's a small boat approaching us from the other steamboat," Kingsley observed.

Cole turned. A yawl with five men in it ranged up alongside the *West Wind*. The four oarsmen on board rested their oars.

"Ahoy, *West Wind*," the man in the sternsheets of the yawl cried up.

"Ahoy," answered Cole, looking down at the man. "Do you need assistance?"

"No, Captain," came the reply. "I'm the clerk of the *John C. Chilton*. We're going to lay up for the night upriver. We thought you'd probably lay up, too, as soon as you're over the bar."

"That's correct."

"Captain McIntyre sends his compliments and has asked me to invite you and your crew and passengers to a dance and party tonight aboard the *Chilton*. Can you come?"

Cole turned to Rebecca. "That boat is probably more like what you're used to on the Mississippi, Miss Kingsley.

She looks like a first class packet. It's traditional to have a party whenever two boats tie up together on the Missouri.''

''These are not the times for frivolity and gaiety, Captain Cole,'' she snapped. Then she spun on her heels and stalked down the boiler deck promenade toward her cabin.

Cole sighed. He called down to the *Chilton's* clerk, ''Delighted at the invitation, sir. Some of us, at least, will attend.''

''Good,'' the man acknowledged. A wide grin spread on his face. ''And is that handsome young lady who was just here included?'' he asked.

Cole shook his head slowly. ''I'm afraid not.''

''A pity,'' the man in the boat said. He waved a parting and motioned the oarsmen to row back. ''Until tonight,'' he called.

Cole waved. Then he looked at Kingsley. ''She would have been the center of the attraction, sir.''

''Yes,'' he agreed. ''Captain, what's the next city?''

''Omaha. Why?''

''Can I send a telegram from there?''

''Yes.''

''How about farther north? Sioux City? Yankton?''

''No,'' Cole told him. ''Omaha's the last telegraph link on the Missouri. We'll be stopping there for provisions, so you can send a telegram then if you wish.''

Kingsley stared at the *Chilton* a moment longer. ''A pity,'' he said. Then he walked away.

Cole wondered why Kingsley seemed so disappointed about the party.

Chapter Five

Omaha was reached by midmorning the next day. Cole got a full load of wood and fresh supplies for the galley and Van Hill took the opportunity to find a saloon on shore. Kingsley and Rebecca both stayed aboard.

Cole never stopped fussing over his boat. He spent only a short time ashore and then was quickly back on the *West Wind*. He was on the forecastle watching O'Brien check the starboard auxiliary engine when Moore came running along the levee toward the steamboat, waving a newspaper in his hand.

"Zach! Zach!" He bounded up the landing stage, panting heavily. "Look at this Omaha paper," he cried. He held out the newspaper so Cole could read the headline. "Richmond's been taken!"

Cole snatched the paper from Moore and began scanning the headlines. O'Brien hopped out of the hold. "Grant's done it," Cole said.

"Well, I'll be," O'Brien declared, reading over Cole's shoulder.

"April third, a couple of days ago," Cole related.

"Hey, Kingsley," Moore shouted toward the boiler deck. "Grant captured Richmond. The war's over!"

"Burt," Cole chided. "You don't have to rub salt in an open wound."

"Okay, okay," the first mate muttered, still beaming.

Even Cole had to grin in spite of himself.

"Captain Cole," Kingsley's tense voice called down from the boiler deck railing.

The men on the forecastle deck looked up, startled at Kingsley's sudden appearance.

"Is it true?" Kingsley demanded.

"Yes, sir, Mr. Kingsley," Cole confirmed. "Says so right here in the paper. Richmond fell."

Very carefully, Kingsley said, "Have Lee and his army been captured as well?"

"No," Cole told him. "No, they haven't."

Kingsley straightened up. "Thank you," he said. He turned on his heels and stalked back to his cabin.

"What do you make of that?" Moore asked. "Does he think the war's not over?"

"He may have a point, Burt," Cole said, reading further. "Says here Lee is retreating to the west. They think he's going to try to link up with Johnston to the south."

"Bah," Moore scoffed. "So then they'll have one big starvin' army instead of two small ones."

"They're still fighting, though," O'Brien pointed out. He was reading the newspaper account as well.

Moore shrugged his shoulders, but he said no more.

Rebecca Kingsley, holding onto her wide-brimmed hat with both hands, strolled up behind Cole where he stood near one of the capstans on the forecastle deck, watching the *West Wind* head toward shore. "This wind is extraordinary, Captain Cole," she said.

Cole jerked his head around. "My mind was elsewhere, Miss Kingsley," he said. "You startled me." But he was hopeful; her tone seemed less hostile.

"I'm sorry," she said. "I see we're stopping at another woodyard."

"Yes, ma'am. Seaton's Woodyard. And then we'll tie up for the rest of the day."

"So early?"

Cole listened to the wind rattling the shutters on the cabin windows and singing in the guy wires supporting the smokestacks. "We present quite a large surface area to this wind, Miss Kingsley. And shallow drafted with no keel like this we'd skitter across the water like a fallen leaf. Steering's almost impossible, so there's a danger we wouldn't be able to avoid snags even if we did see them. Or the wind could blow us right onto shore despite our best efforts to avoid it. Besides that, the wind can sometimes push us back faster than we can travel forward with our engines."

The *West Wind* approached the shore gingerly, slipping sideways with the wind on her flank. As soon as the bow touched bottom, Moore had the landing stage deployed. "Woodpile!" he called. He and the roustabouts marched off the boat.

"Captain," Moore called from the shore. "He wants four dollars a cord. All cottonwood."

"All right," Cole answered. "Better take twenty cords if we can. We burned up a lot of wood fighting this wind."

"Aye aye, sir."

Rebecca, still holding down her hat with a hand, turned to go. "Excuse me, Captain."

Cole wished she would linger awhile. "The wind is getting stronger all the time," he said, just to have something to say. "Sometimes it blows like this for days."

She glanced up as if to look at the wind. "Father will be disappointed," she said simply. Then she turned and walked slowly back toward the forward stairs.

The wind was just as strong the next morning and Cole decided not to try to travel that day, keeping the *West Wind* tied up to the shore. Gusts howled through the uprights and found every crack in every bulkhead. Guy wires hummed, shutters rattled, and tarpaulins on the deck cargo cracked and slapped. The wind picked up dust and sand from the sandbars nearby and scoured the river basin with it and scraped at the *West Wind*.

Cole, poring over a ledger in his office, almost didn't hear the knock on his cabin door. "Come in."

The door opened. Wind blew papers off his desk, and dust scratched his face. He squinted at the grit and tried to hold down his papers as the door was slammed shut.

"Sorry, Captain Cole," Kingsley apologized. "Incredible wind." He sat down on a chair.

"The wind is not your responsibility, Mr. Kingsley. What can I do for you?"

"We are actually in Dakota Territory now, aren't we?"

"Oh, yes. Have been since Sioux City a couple of days ago."

"Well, Captain, with the boat stuck here all day, I don't suppose it would be of any consequence if a party were to go ashore."

Cole shook his head. "No, but hunting will be pretty dull. With this wind you'll have a hard time hitting any game even if you do spot it."

"I wasn't thinking of hunting, Captain. There's an Indian village in sight on the other side of the river."

"That's right. Sioux. All the Missouri River basin north of the Niobrara is Sioux country."

"Well, Captain, would you take the boat across the river—"

Cole shook his head. "I'm sorry. Not in this wind. We'd be completely at its mercy. Besides, if I tied up on the other side of the river, the boat would soon be swamped with Indians, begging, stealing, and making a general nuisance of themselves."

"Are they hostile?"

Cole shrugged. "They're unpredictable. You can't trust them and you can't read them. My advice is to stay away from them."

Kingsley paused. "How about two of your small boats?" he suggested. "I'd use my own men, and a large force would discourage mischief among the Indians."

"You might get stuck there all day," Cole warned. "Getting over there won't be any trouble, but you'll have a terrible time rowing back against that wind."

"I'm willing to take the risk," Kingsley responded, "and I'm most anxious to visit a Sioux village. I've never met any Indians."

Cole stared at Kingsley for a moment, then he shrugged. "Well, it's up to you. The yawls are at your disposal, Mr. Kingsley."

"Thank you, Captain." Kingsley rose and stepped to the door. When he opened it, the wind and dust rushed in again.

Cole slammed the ledger down on top of his papers. He followed Kingsley outside and closed the door behind him, squinting into the gritty blast. "At least go well armed and make it visible," he advised.

"That I shall do," Kingsley answered him as he headed down the stairs.

Cole stopped at the boiler deck railing. Looking down he noticed that Kingsley's men had been assembled on the deck below before Kingsley had spoken to him. Cole was irritated by the man's confidence.

He called down, "Mr. Moore."

Moore popped out from underneath the overhang. "Yes, sir?"

"Launch the yawls, Mr. Moore."

"In this wind?" the first mate asked, incredulous.

"Yes, Mr. Moore," Cole replied. "Launch the yawls. Mr. Kingsley's men will man them."

"Aye aye, sir," a skeptical Moore called back. He shouted for some roustabouts, and the group headed for the hurricane deck, where the yawls were secured, suspended on davits that hinged on the boiler deck above.

Cole scanned Kingsley's party and noted that the men

were indeed well armed. He also noticed they had several boxes and sacks that were obviously going with them.

"Going to do some trading, Mr. Kingsley?" Cole asked. It occurred to Cole that Kingsley must have planned right from the start to visit the Indians.

"Perhaps, Captain," Kingsley replied, looking up. "I've heard that Indians are friendlier if you give them gifts."

"Just because they're polite doesn't mean they're friendly, Mr. Kingsley."

"I'll remember that, Captain."

The yawls were lowered to the water and then towed forward by roustabouts.

"The wind will probably abate after sunset, Mr. Kingsley," Cole said. "If you have to return after dark, I'll make sure the *West Wind's* lights are bright."

"Thank you, Captain," Kingsley responded.

"Good luck," Cole said.

Kingsley nodded acknowledgment. "Thank you, sir."

Chapter Six

Cole, sitting at his office desk, ran his finger down the column of figures in his ledger. "Wood expenses are even higher than last year," he commented.

"It's all this lousy cottonwood," Moore said.

"Yes." The captain turned to O'Brien. "Are the boilers back in operation?"

"We should have minimal pressure soon, Zach," the engineer said. "Having to stop for the wind came at a good time. We'd've had to shut down soon to clean all the mud out of the boilers anyway."

"And the repairs?"

"Done. We replaced that section of leaky steam line just abaft the boilers and I put a brace on the larboard connecting rod."

"Good."

"Say, listen," Moore said, holding up a finger. "Sounds like gunfire."

The three men fell silent. Faintly they heard the crackle of distant rifles.

Cole straightened up in his chair. "Any sign of Kingsley yet?"

"No," answered Moore.

Cole tossed the ledger on the desk, rose, and went to the door; the other two followed. Squinting at the dust that blew in his face, he walked quickly to the railing.

Devlin bounded up the forward stairs. He stopped in front of Cole and saluted.

"Beggin' your pardon, Captain," Devlin said, "but Mr. Kingsley is in trouble." He pointed a mile down the river. "Down there."

Cole, Moore, and O'Brien all looked in the direction indicated.

"Sioux!" Moore exclaimed.

"A bunch of 'em, too," O'Brien added.

"The fool," Cole said. "Looks like he's got himself in a fine fix. I knew I shouldn't have let him go. And what's he doing way down there?"

"Captain," Devlin said, "it don't matter. The yawls are across from us on the river bank. Mr. Kingsley and the others got no way to get back to the boat."

"Serves him right," Cole fumed. "I warned him about that village."

"Captain!" Devlin shouted. "He needs us."

"This wind could blow us straight across the river and strand us, too," Cole snapped. "What good would that do your boss?"

"They might be overrun any minute," warned Devlin.

Cole squinted into the distance. "They seem to be putting up a pretty good resistance. The Indians probably don't have many guns, and precious little ammunition."

"But Captain," Devlin argued, "Miss Rebecca's with him."

Cole jerked his head around. "What! Kingsley didn't say he was taking her with him." Cole's attitude changed abruptly. "All right, Mr. O'Brien, see to your engines. Give me all the steam you can as quick as you can."

"Aye aye, sir." O'Brien ran for the stairs and took them three at a time going down.

"Mr. Moore, go get Mr. Kellogg. Then get below and take the lines in."

"Aye aye, sir," Moore said as he ran aft.

"And send Josh to me, too!" Cole called after him.

Cole turned to Devlin. "I assume your men are prepared for a fight."

"Yes, sir, Captain. I've got about twenty all set."

"All right. Take cover along the larboard side. In this wind I'll have to drop back downriver and then steam up-stream again and beach the boat near Kingsley."

"Yes, sir." Devlin saluted and started hurrying away.

"And when we get there watch out particularly for Miss Kingsley."

"You don't have to say that, Captain," Devlin called over his shoulder. He was gone in an instant, shouting orders as he flew down the stairs.

Kellogg came running over to Cole from his cabin.

"Bob," Cole said. "You take the wheel. Take us down past Kingsley's position. Run the boat stern first downstream though—if we try to turn around we might lose control in this wind."

"Right."

"Then steam back up and beach her as close to Kingsley as you can. Don't wait for my signal, just go as soon as the lines are in."

"Okay, Zach."

Kellogg headed for the stairs to the hurricane deck and the wheelhouse.

Josh came up the stairs and Cole clamped a hand on Josh's big shoulder. "Josh, you're the best swimmer in the crew."

"That's right, suh," the roustabout responded proudly.

Cole pointed across the river to where the *West Wind's* two yawls were beached. "You think you could swim all the way across the river and tow those yawls back out into the channel? Remember, that water's mighty cold."

The roustabout smiled. "That's easy, Cap'n."

"Good man," Cole said, slapping his shoulder. "Now, wait until the boat backs out into the channel, then be on your way."

"Aye aye, Cap'n." Josh hurried for the stairs.

Cole glanced at the forecastle deck and saw Moore supervising two roustabouts hastily coiling rope near the capstans. "Burt, come to my office as soon as you're done there," Cole said. Moore waved an acknowledgment.

Three long blasts on the *West Wind's* steam whistle told Cole that Kellogg was ready. He could already feel the deck vibrating beneath his feet.

Cole hurried to his office and unlocked the chain that ran through the trigger guards of the line of rifles. "Take your pick, Burt," Cole said as Moore came in. He could hear men running on the boiler deck outside.

Moore selected the Sharps and Cole grabbed the Henry. Both men took a box of cartridges from a drawer below the gun rack and Cole went to his desk and retrieved the Colt. He checked to see that each nipple on the cylinder had a copper percussion cap on it, then stuck the pistol in his belt. He grabbed a fistful of paper cartridges for the Colt and stuffed them into his coat pocket.

Van Hill burst into the office. He was carrying a pistol, too. "Looks like a fight," he declared.

"Help yourself to a rifle, Major," Cole said, waving a hand toward the gun rack. "Cartridges and caps in the drawer below."

"Thanks." The officer selected one of the Springfield muskets and grabbed a box of cartridges and caps.

"Let's go," Cole barked.

The three men left the office and descended quickly to the main deck. Devlin approached them. "We're all set, Captain. I've got ten men on the boiler deck and the rest down here. We had to use cargo and furniture for breastwork."

Moore crowded in behind a stack of lumber and Devlin, Cole, and Van Hill wound up together behind a crate.

The *West Wind* was almost abreast of Kingsley's position. Kellogg was doing a good job of a difficult task. With the engines running full astern, he turned the boat this way and that as he struggled to counter the wind's relentless attempts to blow the boat ashore.

Cole checked back up the river, looking for Josh. He saw the man in the middle of the water, powerful strokes of his long dark arms reaching for the opposite shore.

Cole turned his attention to Kingsley and his men. They had formed a defensive position near the shoreline, far from the bluffs in the background. There was little cover for them, just a few low mounds, and Kingsley's men were busy scooping shallow holes in the sandy soil.

The late afternoon sun cast long shadows from the bluffs that stretched beyond the beach, and musket fire on shore created clouds of obscuring, white smoke. But Cole was still able to pick out Rebecca's blue dress pressed to the ground. His jaw clenched tightly.

The *West Wind's* sternwheel stopped, reversed, and then thrashed the muddy river water. The boat's downstream passage was arrested as she headed back upstream, still turned into the wind.

"Devlin," Cole said, turning to the man. "Let the boat come to a complete stop before you open fire. Be ready to grab the people as they get to the boat."

"Yes, sir." Devlin stood up and stepped briskly to the bull rails. He shouted up to the boiler deck. "Murphy!"

A voice called back down. "Yeah, Sergeant?"

Devlin glanced furtively at Cole and Van Hill, and the latter two returned the sudden look of surprise.

"Hmph, Rebels," Van Hill muttered to Cole.

"Ex-Rebels, Major," Cole mumbled back.

"Murphy," Devlin called up again, "wait for my command to fire."

"Yes, sir."

Devlin turned to face the shore and squatted behind the bull rails for cover. The *West Wind's* hull sighed as it rubbed the muddy bottom.

"Get ready, Devlin," Cole said.

The boat stopped. A Sioux bullet plunked into the bulkhead behind Cole. He flinched despite himself.

Devlin jumped up. "Company, in volley!" he called, turning his head from side to side so all could hear. "Ready, aim, fire!"

Twenty muskets blazed in a single thunderous crash.

Van Hill raised his eyebrows and glanced at Cole. "Did you hear that volley? Not a ripple in it," he said in admiration.

Ashore, two Indians fell to the ground and another was knocked off his pony.

"Accurate, too," Cole commented. "Let's help out." He raised his Henry, squinted through the thick cloud of white gunsmoke engulfing the side of the *West Wind*, and squeezed off a shot himself. Then he levered another cartridge into the chamber. Looking to the side he saw Moore open fire with the Sharps.

Van Hill fired his musket, then joined the other men on deck laboriously reloading their own guns. They tore open paper cartridges with their teeth, poured the powder down barrels, and shoved the lead minié balls into the muzzles. Their ramrods slithered and clinked as they rammed the bullets home. Then they cocked the hammers and shoved caps on the firing nipples.

By the time Van Hill was ready to fire again, Cole had fired four more times, taking careful aim with each shot.

Another volley blazed from the side of the *West Wind*. The Indians fell back.

"Fire at will," Devlin shouted. His men started firing. Devlin waved an arm toward those on shore. "Come on!"

Kingsley stood up on the shore and pointed to two men. "You and you, take my daughter to the boat."

The two men jumped to their feet and along with Rebecca splashed into the water and waded out. The Indians started yelling, and advanced again. A few bullets spattered the water around the fleeing people, and several arrows fell close by.

Men on the *West Wind* leaped from their cover and rushed to the side of the boat. They reached down for Rebecca and the two men but Cole barged in and grabbed Rebecca's hands himself. He hoisted her quickly to the deck.

"Thank you, Captain," she said breathlessly.

He helped her to her feet. "Let's get you behind cover on the other side, Miss Kingsley," he said. Putting an arm around her drenched shoulders, he rushed her around the superstructure of the forward storage compartment.

She leaned wearily against the bulkhead, panting rapidly, one hand on her stomach. "You didn't bring the boat a minute too soon, Captain. We were almost out of ammunition."

"You shouldn't have been with them," Cole scolded.

"Captain," she countered, "you have more important things to do right now than lecture me."

"Yes, you're right." He rushed back to the other side of the deck and crouched down next to Van Hill again.

Kingsley sent two more of his men from the beach. They sloshed into the river and struggled toward the boat. An arrow struck one of them in the back when he was no more than ten feet from the boat and he screamed, fell face forward, and started to float away. Two men leaped into the water and grabbed him as others hoisted him aboard.

The other man from the shore clambered aboard, taking cover quickly and adding his own fire to that of the defenders already on the *West Wind*.

Another two men reached the boat, and finally Kingsley and Raasch were the last to leave the shore. One body was left behind on the beach.

Raasch waded swiftly through the water, but Kingsley turned at the water's edge and methodically emptied his pistol at the Sioux. Then he calmly turned around again and headed for the boat. He paid no attention to the bullets and arrows splashing into the water all around him.

"Kingsley, hurry!" Cole shouted impatiently. Kingsley reached the side of the *West Wind*, and he, too, was hoisted aboard by his men. Cole ran to the bow and motioned to Kellogg. "Take her out! Take her out!"

The steamboat's sternwheel flailed the water, and the engines chugged and blasted steam. Slowly, the boat backed off the mud and away from the shore, yawing in the wind.

Angry Indians, screaming defiance, ran into the water and sent arrows and bullets flying toward the retreating steamboat.

Kellogg turned the *West Wind* upstream, and the steamboat pulled away from the Indians. Their firing stopped as the vessel plowed out of range.

Cole rushed over to the rail, where Kingsley was watching the receding shoreline. Van Hill was right after him.

Rebecca had joined her father and thrust a hand around his arm. She was leaning against him.

"Mr. Kingsley," Cole said curtly. "I know the Sioux. They don't favor frontal assaults against heavy firepower. Yet this bunch was doing just that. What did you do to infuriate them?"

"I did nothing."

"Father," Rebecca snapped.

Cole looked at Rebecca and frowned, then quickly looked back at Kingsley. "And why did you take your daughter along?" Cole asked angrily. "That was insane—you gave the Sioux a tempting prize. Did that provoke them?"

"No. I took Rebecca along to show the Sioux that I trusted them."

"But you shouldn't trust them," Cole growled.

Moore interrupted Cole before he could continue. "We picked up Josh and the yawls, Captain," he reported.

Cole nodded a quick acknowledgment. "And another

thing, Mr. Kingsley," Cole went on. "Why did you go traipsing off downriver like that?"

"We had little choice in our path of retreat, Captain," Kingsley said, irritated.

Raasch walked over then to interrupt. "Casualty report, sir," he said to Kingsley.

"Very well, Mr. Raasch. Fitting that you should give it," Kingsley answered.

Cole frowned. "Why is that?" he asked.

"We lost three men dead total, sir," Raasch said. "Two more were wounded and there are two wounded among those who stayed on the boat. But all the wounds are slight."

"Very well."

"That's three men who'd still be alive if you'd listened to my advice, Kingsley," Cole pointed out to him.

Kingsley looked at him angrily. "Don't interfere in things you don't understand, Captain. I am quite capable of taking my own counsel."

"The Sioux were peaceful before you visited them, and now they're hostile. I demand to know what happened at that village."

"You demand?" Kingsley asked indignantly.

"I'll remind you that I am captain of this boat, sir," Cole declared. "And you have endangered it by your folly in going to that village."

"It may be your boat, Captain, but I and my men will go where we please. All thirty of us," he added.

Cole didn't miss the emphasis on the figure.

"Tell him, father," Rebecca urged.

"Daughter, be quiet," Kingsley commanded.

"Tell him what the gallant Mr. Raasch did."

Cole looked apprehensively at Rebecca. "What did Raasch do?"

"Rebecca," Kingsley warned.

"He fired two pistol loads into the Sioux chief's family while they were watching us leave."

Cole's mouth dropped open. Moore whistled.

Rebecca was glaring at Raasch. "He must have killed three or four children as well as the chief's wife and a couple of old men," she said quietly.

Van Hill muttered, "The Sioux from here to Montana will be in an uproar. The entire Dakota Territory will be unsafe for a white man to travel."

"I've had that thought myself," Kingsley said.

Cole gripped the barrel of his Henry tightly and shook his head slowly from side to side. He pointed an angry finger at Raasch. "That man murdered innocent people. And he's started a war. I'm going to turn him over to the Army at—"

"You will turn him over to no one, Captain Cole," Kingsley warned. "That man is my responsibility. We will see that he is treated appropriately. All thirty of us," he repeated once more.

Cole glanced past Kingsley at Devlin and a dozen other men, all of whom still had their weapons ready. He didn't say anything more, only clenched his teeth tightly.

Kingsley stepped to the bull rails and glanced at the passing landscape. "A war out here will be quite minor compared to the slaughter that's been raging for the last four years throughout the South, Captain. A few dead Indians are insignificant."

Cole joined Kingsley at the railing. "I don't think you understand," he said.

"Hmph. Neither did the Sioux," Kingsley snorted. "Not a one of them could understand more than ten words of English."

"What did you expect?" Cole asked. "But what's that got to do with Raasch's actions? What were you trying to say to them?"

Kingsley didn't answer. He nodded toward the shore. "Seems we haven't seen the last of the Sioux."

Cole looked. Along the bluffs was a long line of Sioux,

some on horseback, others walking, but all keeping pace with the *West Wind*.

"Oh no," Cole muttered gloomily. "That's what I was afraid of."

"How far will they follow us, Captain?" Kingsley asked.

"If they're mad enough, they'll follow a boat for hundreds of miles. That's what I'm trying to tell you."

"Then it seems there's more than one way to slice a duck," Kingsley said.

"What are you talking about?" Cole insisted.

Kingsley folded his hands behind his back. "Now, Captain," he went on calmly. "I suggest we take some defensive precautions. Like building some breastwork along the sides?"

"That's the least of our worries, Kingsley," Cole told him angrily. "The river is wide enough to put us out of range most of the time. But we need wood constantly. The Sioux only have to prevent us from getting any wood and they'll stop us without firing a shot. Then they can simply lay siege to us."

"Well, we shall do what must be done, Captain," Kingsley said. He turned on his heel and strode down the deck. "Come along, daughter," he said to Rebecca.

"Yes, father." She caught up to him and clamped a hand around his arm once more.

Raasch headed back toward Devlin and the other men.

Cole watched Kingsley depart. He turned to Moore and Van Hill. "They don't understand," he said.

Van Hill spoke. "Odd, but Kingsley doesn't seem to care that we're stuck on this boat."

"At least he's not likely to want to burn it, is he?" Cole snapped.

Van Hill raised an eyebrow and had to smile. "Well, I guess you have a point there, Captain. On the other hand, I'm sure this action of Raasch's wasn't some random impulse. There was a method to his madness. And, by the way, I was impressed by how you showed Kingsley who was in charge." He actually started to whistle a tune as he turned and continued on his way.

Cole's jaw tightened in humiliation and anger.

"Don't know why he's so cheerful," Moore said, watching the Army officer walk away. Then he turned and looked at the silent line of Sioux moving along the bluffs. "What do we do now?"

Cole turned to watch them. His shoulders slumped. "Well, we can't outrun them. And we're wasting a lot of fuel steaming in this wind. We're going to need every stick we can get our hands on from now on. Let's stop and anchor right where we are."

"And then?"

"Well," Cole sighed after a short pause. "I suggest you break out the spare boiler plates and construct a barricade inside the wheelhouse. That'll be the Sioux's favorite target from now on."

Chapter Seven

T he stacks of cordwood on shore burned fiercely, as did the woodhawk's shack as the *West Wind* nosed gently up against the bank and the landing stage was put out. Kingsley's men charged off the boat with a Rebel yell that made Van Hill turn pale and Cole shudder. The Sioux each fired a single shot and then retreated for the bluffs.

"Just like the Sioux to taunt us like that," a depressed Cole said to Kingsley. "Let us get close enough to the woodyard for us to think they haven't reached it yet, and then fire the wood right in our faces."

"Then they are fools, Captain," Kingsley stated. "Burning woodyards would be a much more effective weapon if they burned them completely. They are letting their emotions cloud their military judgment."

"Well, let's hope they continue that tactic," Cole said.

Ashore, Moore's roustabouts were shoveling dirt onto the crackling cordwood. In the end, the *West Wind* was able to salvage about six cords of wood. But that was far short of a day's requirements.

"What's our next stop, Captain Cole?" Kingsley asked.

"There's a woodyard at Fort Randall," the captain told him. "With the garrison so close to that woodyard, maybe the Sioux won't try to burn it."

Abreast of Fort Randall Cole had the *West Wind's* stern-wheel turn only fast enough to keep the boat from losing headway. The bull rails, larboard railings, and the hurricane deck were studded with spectators, all intently studying the fort on the bluffs.

Cole was at the side of the hurricane deck, near the wheelhouse. He was using a telescope. A large band of Sioux were sniping at the fort and at the inevitable clutter of shacks and huts that grew up around any frontier post.

"Fort Randall?" Kingsley asked, coming up to Cole. Raasch was with Kingsley.

"Yes," Cole confirmed, lowering the telescope. "And you can see the results of Mr. Raasch's work," he said acidly, glaring at Raasch. "Mr. Kingsley, that fort's in danger, and you've got fighting men," Cole said.

"Doesn't look like much of an attack to me," Raasch observed indifferently.

"No," Kingsley agreed. "And after we help drive the Sioux off, then what, Captain? We'd be cooped up here right along with those soldiers. You still want to get to Fort Benton, don't you?"

Cole had to admit that he did.

Raasch spoke up. "How about the wood?"

"No chance," Cole said. "The wood is still there, but the fort hasn't kept the Sioux far enough away from the woodyard. The Indians are well protected on that bluff. Even your men won't be able to keep them from shooting down at my roosters as they gathered in the wood."

"May I suggest then, Captain," Kingsley said, "that we stop discussing the situation and move on. We are wasting valuable wood just sitting here like this. How far to the next woodlot?"

Cole pushed in the tubes of his telescope. "There's usually a big sandbar just upriver from the fort, and it often collects a lot of driftwood. We'll check it out." He turned to the wheelhouse. "Mr. Kellogg, take us to the Fort Randall Bar," he called.

Kellogg beached the *West Wind* in the lee of the Fort Randall Bar. Cole was relieved to see a sizable rack of driftwood on the bar consisting of a jumble of old trees bleached white and barkless and new trees freshly dug up by the rising Missouri and deposited there.

Half of Kingsley's men trooped off and took up positions at the edges of the bar while the other half manned the railings on the steamboat. Roustabouts deployed with axes and saws. Half of them chopped and sawed while the other half carried wood back to the steamboat, wading through the water and throwing the limbs and trunk sections onto the deck. Other roustabouts tried to stack the oddly shaped pieces of wood into some semblance of order.

"This will help," Cole said to Kingsley. "But the best wood has already been picked up by other boats. All we're getting is wet logs and corkscrew-shaped stuff that'll take up a lot of space in the fireboxes but give us little heat."

"I'm sure there'll be more," Kingsley answered confidently.

Kingsley's remark was dense, Cole thought; Kingsley had never been up the Missouri before. He looked at the Sioux, high on the bluffs, out of rifle range, silently watching the *West Wind's* operations.

Kingsley followed his glance. "Those Indians are persistent," he said admiringly.

"Like vultures," Cole said.

"After death has been a constant companion for a long time, Captain," Kingsley said, "you tend to ignore it. Soon you won't even notice those savages." He turned and walked away.

Cole didn't answer, but he was sure he'd never get used to those Sioux perched on the bluffs.

Cole held the wheel hard over, then spun it back to straighten out the boat in a violent maneuver. Holding his breath, he watched the sunken tree, detectable only by the telltale ripples marring the surface of the Missouri, glide past perilously close to the side of the *West Wind*. He let out his breath.

"Captain," Rebecca called from outside the wheelhouse.

Cole turned and smiled at the pretty young woman standing at the foot of the steps. "Miss Kingsley," he said.

"May I join you?" she asked.

"Please do," he said eagerly.

She came up the steps and went to the forward windows. "Such dreary scenery, Captain Cole. Just mile after mile of grassy hills and crumbling, sandy bluffs. And the bluffs away from the river's edge are so high, you can't see anything beyond," she sighed.

"I'm afraid it looks the same beyond the hills, Miss Kingsley."

"Have you done much exploring away from the river, Captain?" she asked.

Cole shook his head. "I stay as near the water as I can. No self-respecting steamboat captain is willing to do any more walking than absolutely necessary."

"Ah, I see," she said with a smile. "Oh, look at all those deer," she exclaimed. She pointed to the side.

Cole followed her pointing. "Those aren't deer; they're antelope. Pronghorns."

"Must be a hundred of them," she commented in awe.

"And good eating, too," Cole added.

"Any chance of getting some for supper?" she asked.

"Thanks to Mr. Raasch," Cole said with deliberation, "the boat's hunter is either dead with his scalp gone or he's cleared out of the territory."

Rebecca paused. "I hope it's the latter," she said at last.

"Miss Kingsley," Cole said. "I don't know how your father can excuse the killing of innocent people and the start of—''

Rebecca interrupted heatedly. ''Sometimes circumstances compel us to accept people and actions which we would not otherwise accept.''

''What circumstances?'' Cole asked.

But Rebecca turned her head away. ''I see we're catching up to another steamboat,'' she said.

Cole knew she was deliberately changing the subject. ''Yes,'' he said sullenly. ''Its smoke has been visible for a long time. There's a telescope in the corner. You can probably read her name on the wheelhouse.''

Rebecca spotted the telescope. She brought it to the forward window and squinted through the eyepiece. ''The *Pathfinder*,'' she announced. ''And she's stuck on a bar.''

''The bars around Pocahontas Island.''

''And we'll have to spar again; too?'' Rebecca said.

''Yes. It's always too shoal around the island. Matter of fact—'' He leaned over and called into the speaking tube. ''Mr. O'Brien, please have soundings taken.''

The soundings were soon being called.

''Four feet!''

''It's pretty shallow already,'' Rebecca commented.

''Uh-huh.''

''Four feet scant!''

''Three and a half feet!''

The *West Wind* lurched, jerked ahead and then slowly came to a stop.

''Stuck,'' she pronounced.

Cole called into the speaking tube. ''Shut off the main engines, Mr. O'Brien. I want to conserve as much steam as possible.'' He turned to Rebecca. ''Would you like to watch the sparring from the hurricane deck, Miss Kingsley?''

''All right,'' she said.

Cole led her out of the wheelhouse. They walked forward and met Kingsley coming up the starboard stairs.

"Captain Cole," Kingsley said.

Cole and Rebecca stopped. "Yes?" Cole said.

"Captain, I noticed that steamboat up ahead. I was wondering if we were going to catch up to her before dark."

"I doubt it, Mr. Kingsley," Cole said. "She's almost done sparring and we've just started. There are a good many hours of daylight left. She can put on a lot of miles yet today."

"I see." Kingsley looked at Rebecca. "Rebecca, I don't think you should be out in this hot sun. Come along."

Cole thought Kingsley's remark odd. It was actually a cloudy day.

Rebecca squinted up at the sky. "You're right, father," she concluded. nodding politely to Cole. "Some other time, Captain."

Cole nodded. "Of course, Miss Kingsley." Kingsley took her by the arm and led her toward the stairs.

Cole watched them leave. The sound of the capstan engines bursting into life interrupted his thoughts, and he walked the rest of the way to the forward edge of the hurricane deck. Below, he could see that Moore had already deployed the spars, and the capstans were winding up line.

Several of Kingsley's men started gathering near the forward hatches. They all seemed to be watching Moore on deck and O'Brien in the hold. Moore was beginning to look around uneasily. Cole's scalp cringed when he realized that Kingsley's men had their rifles with them.

Cole turned sharply about and hurried for the stairs, stopping short before he turned to descend. Kingsley was coming up the stairs with two of his men. Both were carrying rifles. And both the rifles had bayonets affixed.

Chapter Eight

"Zach!" Moore's warning was followed quickly by the report of a musket.

"Captain Cole," Kingsley said, reaching the head of the stairs. "There's no longer any need for pretense. I am taking over—"

Cole put an angry boot into Kingsley's chest and shoved hard. With a grunt and a futile grab for Cole's foot, Kingsley sailed backwards down the stairs.

The man at Cole's left shouted, "Colonel!" as he watched his commander crash to the deck below. Cole clamped a strong hand on the man, spun him around, and pitched him down the stairs, too.

But the other soldier yelled and lunged with his bayoneted rifle. The blade sliced across Cole's side as he twisted aside.

Cole yelped at the sudden pain, and, grimacing, grabbed the rifle barrel with both hands and yanked hard as he continued to spin. The soldier's momentum carried him around, and Cole kept pulling the rifle in a wide arc. The Rebel refused to let go, and stumbled forward until Cole swung him right off the hurricane deck.

The man screamed. He released the rifle and pumped the air with both arms and legs until he hit the water flat on his stomach with a resounding slap.

A rifle fired at the foot of the stairs and Cole sucked in his breath when he heard a minié ball zip past his ear.

"Don't shoot him!" Kingsley roared. "I need him alive. Get him!"

"Yes, sir." The soldier charged up the stairs again.

Cole swung the rifle he was holding around, pointed it down the stairs, cocked the hammer all the way back and pulled the trigger. The report was loud and sharp, and a white cloud of smoke burst down the stairs. The soldier pitched backwards, knocking Kingsley down again.

Cole heard more shots below, but the bullets weren't aimed at him. More of Kingsley's men appeared.

"After him," Kingsley shouted. "I want him alive."

Cole hurled the rifle down the stairs like a spear, but the men coming up jumped aside.

Cole spun around and ran for the other side of the deck. At the edge of the hurricane deck he dropped to a sitting position, grabbed a stanchion, and swung himself down to land on the railing below.

He hit the deck running and ducked into the last cabin on the larboard side, closing the door quickly. He rushed to the inside cabin door and opened it slightly but saw no one in the salon. He ran across to his own office and burst in. Rushing to his desk, Cole yanked open the upper right hand drawer and reached for his Navy Colt. It was missing.

"Looking for this?" came a voice said from behind him.

Cole whirled and saw her standing in the corner of the cabin. Rebecca was holding the gun with both hands, pointing it squarely at his chest.

He took a step toward her, his focus darting between the Colt's bore and the woman's eyes. "Ever shoot a man in cold blood, Miss Kingsley?" he asked.

"If it's a Yankee, I'd enjoy it," she replied. "There'll never be enough dead Yankees to pay for the death of my mother."

Cole took another step closer. "I don't think you could do it, Miss Kingsley, put a bullet through my heart and watch the blood gush all over the deck."

Rebecca cocked the hammer. "Try me, Captain." She raised the pistol slightly, aiming now at Cole's head.

Cole stopped. Boots thumped on the deck outside. He stared at the pistol, then at Rebecca's eyes again. They had the same fire he'd seen during the confrontation at the dinner table.

Suddenly the outside cabin door burst open and Kingsley and three soldiers rushed in. "Hold it!" Three bayoneted rifles pointed at Cole. "You are my prisoner, Captain Cole," Kingsley declared.

Cole sagged. "I guess we'll both wonder if you could've pulled that trigger, Miss Kingsley," he said. He yanked a handkerchief out of a pocket and stuffed it inside his shirt to stanch the flow of blood from the wound in his side. It wasn't very painful or deep, but it was messy.

Rebecca glared at him. She handed the pistol to her father.

"Well done, daughter," Kingsley said. "I'm proud of you." He let the hammer down and tucked the pistol in his belt, then turned to Cole. "Captain, your keys, please." He held out a hand.

Cole made no move to comply.

Kingsley snapped his fingers. "Come, come, Captain," he insisted with irritation. "Do we have to club you senseless to get them?"

Cole glanced at the soldiers; they looked eager to do just that. "All right." He stuck a hand into his vest pocket and pulled out the keys to the gun rack and the strongbox.

"Thank you," Kingsley said, accepting them. He turned and opened the padlock securing the rifles. After pulling the chain through the guards, he lifted Cole's Henry rifle from its place and examined it covetously, caressing the stock and receiver. "Things would have turned out differently for us at Gettysburg if we'd had a thousand of these. But . . . ."

Kingsley went to the closet, opened the door, and knelt down. Leaning the rifle against the doorjamb, he unlocked and opened the strongbox. He stirred the contents with a hand, examining everything. "The Confederacy can buy a lot of guns with this," he told Cole. He let the lid drop, locked the box again, and stood up.

Devlin appeared at the door. "Colonel," he said, saluting. "The boat is secured. All resistance has been subdued."

"Very well, Sergeant," Kingsley acknowledged. "Have all the prisoners other than roustabouts brought to the forecastle deck. I wish to speak to them."

"Yes, sir." The sergeant saluted again and left.

Kingsley picked up the Henry and waved toward the door. "Down to the main deck, Captain." A bayonet prick in the small of his back persuaded Cole to comply.

The group left Cole's office and headed for the stairs. Rebecca stopped at the boiler deck railing to watch the proceedings below, while Kingsley, Cole, and the soldiers descended the stairs.

On the forecastle deck they found the crew and Van Hill assembled. Moore was lying on the deck, one hand clutching his side. Blood ran down his neck.

Cole bent down over his first mate. "Looks like they worked you over pretty good, Burt."

"Sorry, Zach," Moore gulped, swallowing blood. "Five I could've handled, but six was just one too many." He saw the blood on Cole's coat. "Looks like they got you, too."

"Just a scratch," Cole said. He patted Moore on the shoulder. "You did better than I did, Burt. Thanks for trying."

Cole rose and glanced down the row. O'Brien was standing next to Kellogg. Neither of them showed signs of a fight, but Van Hill's tunic was torn and was missing several buttons, and its sleeve had come loose at the shoulder. The major's hair was disheveled, and he sniffled at blood trickling from his nose. He looked at Cole with a triumphant I-told-you-so smirk and Cole avoided his eyes.

Billy, the decksweep, was at the end of the line. He

looked sullen and angry, and Cole guessed that the gash on his cheekbone may have had something to do with it. A pretty spunky kid.

Cole looked toward the *Pathfinder*, only to see her railings lined with people staring at the *West Wind*, trying to figure out what all the shooting had been about.

Raasch came up to Kingsley and saluted. "Sir," Raasch began, "there's been no damage to the boat. The engines are intact."

"Good, good," Kingsley said. "Casualties?"

"One dead, sir; Moore killed Private Walters with a bayonet. And Captain Cole put a minié ball into Private Merry's stomach; he may not live."

"Other wounded?"

"Four, sir. Private Solomons was shot in the arm by Major Van Hill. Private Brace has a broken arm, Corporal Wyndam is badly cut up, and Private Rowe has a couple of cracked ribs from hitting the water."

"Very well," Kingsley said, facing the line of prisoners. "Gentlemen," he began, "this steamboat has been seized by the Confederate States Army. No harm will come to you as long as you cooperate. But I am prepared to take drastic measures. These are desperate times, and desperate action is required."

"Are you going to burn my boat?" Cole asked. His voice was angry, and was tightened by despair.

"Like that boat in St. Joe?" Moore added.

"No, not like the boat I burned in St. Joseph," Kingsley answered.

Now Moore smirked at Cole. Cole was feeling mighty foolish.

"I'm going to use the *West Wind*," Kingsley said. "My immediate need is to catch that steamboat yonder before she gets off this bar."

"You'll burn her if you catch her, though, won't you?" Cole said.

"Yes," Kingsley confirmed. "Her and any other steamboats we encounter."

"Colonel Kingsley," Van Hill said. "I fail to see any legitimate military objective in destroying steamboats on the Upper Missouri. Their destruction can have no effect on the war, particularly at this late date."

"The commerce of the United States must be destroyed wherever it is found," Kingsley declared. "The exact location is immaterial."

"Are you daft?" Cole exclaimed. "You think you're one of those Confederate raiders like Semmes on the *Alabama*, floating around in the middle of the Atlantic? Kingsley, we're an ungainly, slow-moving steamboat on a shallow, bar-ridden river. There's no empty ocean to disappear into, no fog banks to hide in."

"Surprise is in our favor, Captain," Kingsley said.

"Surprise?" Cole repeated. "News of what you've done will spread like wildfire along the whole Missouri."

"No it won't," Kingsley argued. "There's no telegraph above Omaha, remember."

Cole snorted. "A man on a good horse can reach all the forts on the Missouri long before we do. Why, a man can simply walk up the river faster than we can travel, what with all the loops and bends in the river's course."

"Ah, but no one is likely to be traveling along the Missouri except by boat for awhile, remember that, too?" He nodded toward the Indians on the high bluffs.

He smiled. "I must admit that Captain Raasch's method of enlisting the Indians in our cause was rather unorthodox, but I was always skeptical that I'd be able to recruit the Sioux, even if they had understood what I was trying to ask."

"But the Sioux are angry at you, too, now," Cole said.

Kingsley shrugged. "Doesn't matter. Captain Raasch very effectively made sure that communication ashore would be very difficult at best."

"You condone murder?"

"It wasn't murder," the colonel said. "Those Indians were merely casualties of war. Can that be any worse than Yankees shelling our cities and decimating civilian populations? Killing my wife?"

Van Hill interrupted. "The forts have field artillery, Kingsley. They'll blow this boat out of the water."

Kingsley scoffed. "The Union Army hasn't left but the vilest, most wretched soldiers out here. I doubt any of them will be sober enough to hit us, even if they do decide to fire on us."

Van Hill was silent. He knew Kingsley was probably right. The lethargy of the soldiers was matched only by the spinelessness of most of the officers in the forts. If only he were ashore and not on the boat.

"Kingsley, this is ridiculous," Cole declared. "There's not a half dozen boats on the whole Upper Missouri."

"Burning the steamboats is only incidental to our relieving them of their gold," Kingsley said.

"These boats don't have much money on them," Cole said.

"Not going up the river," Kingsley admitted. "But dust and nuggets have been stockpiling all winter at Fort Benton, waiting for the first steamboat to reach the head of navigation. There must be well over a million dollars waiting up there. And it'll all be loaded onto the first boat coming back downstream, and she'll float right into our laps."

Cole realized that Kingsley was right about that. "And then?" he asked.

"Then we'll march overland to Texas from Fort Benton."

Cole glanced up at Rebecca at the boiler deck railing. "She's going to march all the way to Texas?"

"She is willing to make any sacrifice necessary," Kingsley said. "When we get to Texas, the gold will be sent overseas. Our cotton is useless; not enough gets through the blockade to make much difference. But gold is easily slipped through Mexico and on to Europe. And the Europeans will sell us anything for gold. Guns, ammunition, uniforms, shoes for our men."

"Hmph. The war will be over by the time you hike all the way down to Texas," Van Hill said.

"The war will last a long time, Major," Kingsley insisted. "But time is precious, and I've wasted more of it than I should have in talking to you." He turned around. "Captain Raasch, raise our flag."

"Yes, sir." Raasch in turn looked at two soldiers standing at the foot of the jackstaff at the bow. One carried a neatly folded flag under his arm. "Lower the Union flag," Raasch commanded. The stars and stripes fell to the deck, and one of the soldiers kicked it overboard.

"Unfortunately," Kingsley said to Cole, "We do not have our national colors. We'll have to use our beloved battle flag instead. But it will be a pleasure to no longer sail under that accursed banner of yours."

"Present arms!" Raasch shouted. All the soldiers on the deck snapped to attention. "Raise the flag!"

A Confederate battle flag, jagged, frayed, and faded, zipped up the halyards to the top of the jackstaff. It snapped full open in the stiff breeze, displaying its red field and starstudded blue St. Andrew's cross.

Cole looked from the flag to Kingsley. The colonel stood stiffly, saluting, his face stern and defiant and proud. Beyond him Cole saw Rebecca at the boiler deck railing. Her eyes this time had the fire of pride instead of hate.

On the *Pathfinder*, consternation had exploded at the sight of the Rebel flag.

Kingsley smiled in satisfaction.

But Van Hill said, "You'll have more trouble taking that boat than you think, Kingsley."

"Hm?" Kingsley asked. "How so?"

Van Hill nodded toward the *Pathfinder*. "They've got troops aboard. Must be a contingent for one of the forts."

Now everybody on the *West Wind's* forecastle deck looked over at the *Pathfinder*. Though not noticed before, blue-coated Union soldiers were now swarming over the deck cargo and lining the railings. Officers marshalled them into defensive positions.

"And I think there's more of them than there are of you," Van Hill pointed out triumphantly.

Kingsley smiled. "The odds are still in our favor."

"Colonel," Cole said urgently. "A gun battle between these two boats would be disastrous. Bullets will go right through these bulkheads."

"Captain Cole," Kingsley said, "I do not intend to be on this river very long, but while I am on it, I intend to rule it." He turned. "Captain Raasch, break out the battery."

"Yes, sir."

"Battery?" Van Hill repeated.

Raasch started barking orders, and most of Kingsley's men hustled aft, leaving a few to guard the prisoners. The wagons on the after deck were unloaded. The wagon boxes torn down, and the wheel assemblies removed. Two big crates were broken open and the packing and top layer of mining supplies tossed aside to reveal the gleaming bronze barrels of two field guns.

"Twelve-pounder Napoleons," Van Hill gasped.

"With a plentiful supply of shot, shell, canister, and powder," Kingsley added.

Each cannon tube was affixed to a special cradle by means of its trunnions, and the cradles were mounted on the wagon wheel assemblies. The cannons were wheeled forward to the forecastle, where a breastwork of sorts was quickly being built from the knocked-down wagon boxes, with the cargo of lumber for bulwarks. Even using skeleton gun crews, the two field guns were loaded rapidly.

Kingsley laughed. "Well, well. Look at your brave boys

in blue now, gentlemen,'' he taunted. ''Seems like they'd rather take their chances with the Sioux than with me.''

Soldiers were pouring over the sides of the *Pathfinder* and dropping into the water. They waded for shore, rifles and packs held above their heads.

''They'll spread the alarm, Kingsley,'' Cole pointed out. ''There are too many of them for that band of Sioux to stop.''

Kingsley shrugged. ''Perhaps. Right now I've got to get to the *Pathfinder* before she gets off this bar.''

''You'll have to do a lot of sparring,'' Cole said hopefully.

Kingsley smiled condescendingly. ''Captain Raasch,'' he ordered. ''Lighten the boat. Be quick about it.''

''Yes, sir,'' Raasch replied.

All the hatches were opened and the roustabouts were sent into the hold. Lines were formed and cargo was removed from the hold and tossed overboard. Freight from the forward storage compartment on the main deck was also jettisoned.

Gradually the *West Wind's* draft decreased. Those aboard her could feel the current start to work the boat loose.

Kingsley addressed the prisoners again. ''Mr. Kellogg, I have no further need of your services or that of the deck-sweep. You will both be placed in the hold.''

''The hold?'' gasped Kellogg. His voice trembled.

''Colonel Kingsley,'' begged Cole. ''If this boat hits a snag, she'll sink like a rock. There'll be no chance for anybody in the hold to get out. They'll drown.''

''This is war,'' Kingsley said. ''Mr. O'Brien,'' he continued, ''will you operate the engines, or do you wish to join the others in the hold?''

O'Brien wet his lips. He looked at Cole. ''Captain . . . ''

Cole nodded reluctantly.

''I'll run the engines, Kingsley,'' O'Brien said. ''But under protest.''

"Of course." Kingsley stepped in front of where Moore lay. Looking down, he said, "Mr. Moore, it is too bad you are not on our side. You killed one of my men, but you were merely doing your duty, and I never fault a man for doing his duty, particularly when he does it so well."

Moore said nothing.

"It would please me if you would continue in your duties aboard the boat, if you are physically able to. Or would you prefer the company of Mr. Kellogg and the decksweep in the hold?"

"I don't want to drown like a rat, Kingsley," the first mate said reluctantly. He started to get up, and Cole helped him. "I'll handle the roustabouts."

"Thank you." Kingsley stepped in front of Van Hill. "Frankly, Major Van Hill, I was surprised at how forcefully you resisted capture. Perhaps Chickamauga was an aberration. Since you are an officer I do not want to confine you in the hold. You may have the run of the boat, if you do not try to escape or try to sabotage the engines or the boilers."

"You can't get rid of me, Colonel," Van Hill asserted. "I'm going to stay until you're stopped or I'm dead."

Kingsley smiled. "Noble sentiments. Would you prefer the hold?"

"I do not wish to risk death in the hold; such a sacrifice would be pointless. I want to stay alive so that I can stop you."

"That's no more than an officer's duty. Fair enough, but you will be watched constantly."

Kingsley moved on to stand in front of Cole. "Well, Captain, the boat needs a skilled pilot. My daughter reports that you consider yourself the best pilot on the Upper Missouri."

"I refuse to pilot," Cole announced. "And with no one to pilot the boat, you're not going anywhere."

Kingsley smiled once more. "Oh, someone will pilot,

Captain. And I think it would be inappropriate to incarcerate a steamboat captain in his own hold.''

Cole eyed Kingsley suspiciously. ''I have the run of the boat, too?''

''Why, yes,'' Kingsley said. He looked around. ''Captain Raasch, show the prisoners to their cell.''

''In you go,'' Raasch commanded. He pointed to the hold.

Billy and Kellogg were sent down. Kellogg stopped halfway into the hold and looked over at Cole. His face was pale. ''Captain—''

But Raasch kicked him on the shoulder and Kellogg fell the rest of the way into the hold.

''Don't worry, Bob,'' Cole called after him.

The *West Wind* started to drift, though still rubbing the mud with her hull. She began to turn sideways to the current.

''Hm, let's see,'' Kingsley deliberated. He scanned the soldiers still working to construct the breastwork. ''Private Loomis.''

A young soldier, thin to the point of emaciation, looked up. ''Sir?''

''Private Loomis, you will take the wheel and pilot this boat.''

The private's eyes grew large, and he looked up at the wheelhouse far above his head. ''Steer the steamboat?'' Horror crept into his face. ''I don't know nothin' 'bout steerin' a steamboat, Colonel. This is the first time I even been on one.''

''Nevertheless, I want you to steer. Pick up your rifle and go to the wheelhouse. Hurry! The boat is beginning to drift.''

''Yes, sir.'' Nervously the youth walked over and took his rifle from where it leaned against a stationary. Slowly he trudged up the stairs to the boiler deck.

Cole stepped closer to Kingsley. ''Kingsley, you can't

do that,'' he growled. ''That boy'll put us on a snag for sure. Kellogg and Billy will drown.''

''Yes, and your boat will be lost. A pity, but what can I do?'' Kingsley held up his hands in a gesture of helplessness. ''This is war.''

''If the boat sinks, what happens to your plans for getting gold for the Confederacy?'' Cole asked.

''The plans will have to be changed, Captain,'' Kingsley admitted. ''But I can't get any gold sitting here. I must take the risk of sinking this boat.''

Cole nervously watched Loomis turn the corner of the cabin superstructure.

''Zach,'' Moore muttered. ''We're free of the bottom.''

''Which will it be, Captain? Your boat or—'' Kingsley nodded toward the *Pathfinder*. ''—that boat?''

Cole watched Loomis climb forlornly toward the hurricane deck. Cole was desperate. The boat would probably be safer just drifting by itself than with the young boy piloting it. And what about Kellogg and Billy in the hold?

''Colonel,'' Raasch said, ''the hold's empty now except for the prisoners. We only kept necessary provisions and ammunition in the main deck storage compartment.''

''Very well. Cover all the hatches and weight them down with boxes of shot so the prisoners can't get out.''

Cole glared at Kingsley. ''You've got to give them at least some chance if we sink.''

Kingsley ignored Cole and turned to the remaining prisoners on deck. ''Mr. Moore, you will please have the spars secured. They're dragging, and we don't need them anymore.''

''All right,'' Moore said sullenly.

''Mr. O'Brien, please return to your engines.''

O'Brien nodded reluctantly, but he headed aft quickly.

''Captain?'' Kingsley asked. He saw that Cole's eyes were fixed on Loomis as the soldier gingerly put his hands on the wheel of the *West Wind*.

"All right, Kingsley," Cole spat out.

"Thank you, Captain," Kingsley said. "Take us to a short distance from the *Pathfinder*. We'll anchor there."

Cole broke into a run for the stairs.

"And Captain," Kingsley called after him. "If you strand us or sink us, I will shoot you!"

Cole took the stairs three steps at a time. He didn't have time to more than glower at Rebecca as he rushed around the corner of the cabin superstructure, bounding up the remaining stairs and racing for the wheelhouse.

"Get out of here," Cole barked.

Loomis's pale face brightened. "Yes, sir!" he agreed eagerly. "Thank you, sir."

With no more than a glance downstream Cole spun the wheel and rang for full speed.

The sternwheel started churning water. Slowly the *West Wind's* head came around, and she again pointed up the Missouri rather than athwart it. The boat gained headway, and Cole steered a course parallel to the other steamboat.

Van Hill came panting up the wheelhouse steps. "Cole," he gasped, "smash her!"

"And kill the men in the hold?" Cole said.

"Can't you pick out a snag in shallow enough water so she'd sink without filling the hold?" an exasperated Van Hill asked.

"Snags are where you find them," Cole snapped. He glared at Van Hill. "Besides, this is my boat. I've worked too hard just to sink her deliberately."

Van Hill pointed to the *Pathfinder*. "But Kingsley's going to burn that steamboat."

"Like Kingsley says," Cole said, "it's that boat or this one, and there's nothing I can do about it. In fact, since the *Pathfinder's* still stuck, Kingsley could simply row over to her and torch her anyway. Or destroy her with cannonfire from right here."

"How can you calculate like that?" Van Hill snarled.

Cole growled back. "The war's almost over. I don't want to sacrifice anything this close to the end. The *West Wind* is everything I've got. And don't forget about Kellogg and Billy."

"Why, you'd help these Rebels sink every steamboat we come across," Van Hill said in astonishment.

"There won't be any more steamboats, Major," Cole declared. "As soon as word of the *Pathfinder* gets out, every steamboat ahead of us will make sure they stay ahead of us, way ahead of us."

Angrily, Van Hill strode to the forward window.

"Besides," Cole added. "He said he'd shoot me if I even stranded the boat."

"He can't shoot you, Captain," Van Hill said. "He needs you to pilot. Call his bluff."

"Easy enough for you to bluff with my life."

"He's not the kind to just shoot a man in cold blood."

"I'm not willing to take that chance," Cole shouted. "He said he was desperate. There's going to be a steamboat burned here soon no matter what I do. So I'm going to make sure it's not mine."

Van Hill stormed out of the wheelhouse and headed for the boiler deck stairs.

Cole fumed and gripped the wheel spokes tighter, turning the wheel slightly to correct the boat's course. He hated to be a part of burning a steamboat; no riverman liked to see a steamboat burned or destroyed. But the thought of all those years of taking so much guff from clerks and mates and captains and pilots, years of sweat, risk, and struggle, left him no choice.

No, he would not simply throw his boat away.

Chapter Nine

The lightened *West Wind* glided over sandbars that all of Cole's instinct told him should have grounded her. They would reach the *Pathfinder* in short order, and Cole felt sick at heart.

One of Kingsley's two field guns fired, belching flame and a huge cloud of smoke that rolled over the water. A solid shot splashed expertly just in front of the bow of the *Pathfinder*.

The stars and stripes on the *Pathfinder's* jackstaff fluttered to the deck, and white flags blossomed along the railings.

Kingsley motioned to Cole, and the captain rang the bell to stop the engines. Moore had the two anchors at the bow tossed overboard, and the *West Wind* drifted backward until the anchor chains went taut.

Kingsley sent Raasch and a detail of six men in one of the *West Wind's* yawls over to the *Pathfinder*. While they were gone, crews remained at the field guns. By the time Raasch returned with the steamboat's captain, Cole had raced to the main deck. He knew the captain of the *Pathfinder*, and wanted to explain things to him, though he didn't know what he could really say.

"Cole," his counterpart called angrily as he climbed from the yawl to the *West Wind's* deck.

"Captain Carpenter," Cole said quickly, "I want you to know—"

"Cole, are you crazy?" Carpenter declared. "Throwing

in with a bunch of die-hard Rebels fighting their own private war? Why, you always said the South was foolish to fight in the first place. And now you're going to burn my boat? Why?''

Kingsley interrupted. ''In all fairness to Captain Cole, I must tell you that he is not providing the *West Wind* of his own free will, Captain Carpenter.''

Carpenter looked Kingsley up and down. ''And who are you?''

''I am Colonel Thaddius Kingsley, Third Tennessee Volunteers, Confederate States Army.''

''Confederate Army?'' Carpenter scoffed. ''You're nothing but a bunch of outlaws and pirates.''

''Carpenter,'' Cole broke in. He was desperate to explain. ''The colonel here threw some of my crew into the hold. If I don't cooperate, he'll pilot the boat himself and—''

Carpenter looked shocked. ''The hold?'' He glared at Kingsley. ''Even the best pilots hit snags once in a while. That hold will flood like that.'' He snapped his fingers. ''They'll drown like rats. It's murder.''

''It is war, Captain,'' Kingsley argued.

''War? What war? The war's over, everybody knows that.''

''The war is not over,'' Kingsley snapped. ''Richmond may be taken, but we still have armies in the field.''

''Well, mighty few,'' Carpenter retorted. ''And small ones to boot.''

''Lee's army may be small,'' Kingsley said, his back stiffening, ''but his troops are the finest body of—''

''Lee? Why, Lee surrendered a week ago.''

''What?'' gasped Kingsley, staggered. There was a murmur of concern among his men.

''Are you sure?'' Cole asked. ''How'd you hear about it?''

''Why, at Fort Randall,'' the other man said. ''Didn't they tell you about it?''

"No," Cole informed him. "We didn't stop at Fort Randall. The fort was under attack by Sioux when we passed it."

"Funny. Those Sioux were real quiet when we were at the fort, but they sure have been a plague ever since then. Wonder what got them so hoppin' mad."

Cole gave Kingsley a smirk. "The good colonel here could—"

Kingsley interrupted. "Do you have any confirmation of Lee's surrender? A newspaper, a letter, anything?" Kingsley insisted.

"No, I don't have anything like that."

"Hmph. Well, no matter," Kingsley declared. "Even if Lee was captured, which I doubt, the war would go on. Lee isn't the Confederacy."

"But, Colonel—"

"Captain Carpenter," Kingsley said, raising a hand. "I do not intend to debate further. I have a mission to accomplish and time is precious."

"Mission? Some lunatic scheme to save the Confederacy by burning a few steamboats a thousand miles away from the nearest fighting?"

"Before I burn your steamboat, Captain, all valuables aboard the *Pathfinder*, particularly those in your strongbox, will be confiscated and turned over to me."

"But that's civilian property."

"So was that of the people of Atlanta and Savannah and Richmond and dozens of other Southern cities razed by the Yankee horde!"

"But—"

"Silence! The North makes no distinction between military and civilian, and neither will I. You will transfer all of your passengers and crew to the *West Wind*. Any female passengers will have the freedom of the boat, but you, your crew, and all male passengers will join the others in the hold."

Carpenter cringed. He looked at Cole. "Pilot well, Captain Cole."

"All the cordwood aboard your vessel will be transferred to this one. Also, all guns, ammunition, food, and other provisions. Roustabouts from both boats will be employed in jettisoning your cargo."

"What for? You said you were going to burn the boat."

"Only after I move it to an appropriate spot and sink it to block the channel. I intend the *West Wind* to be the last boat to Fort Benton for quite a while."

"Block the channel? Hah! You don't know the power of the Missouri, mister. Why, in two days the river will have dug a new channel around my boat."

"Enough talking," Kingsley ordered. "Captain Raasch will take you back to the *Pathfinder*. He will see that my orders are carried out. Captain Cole, back to the wheelhouse. Bring the *West Wind* directly alongside the *Pathfinder*."

"But listen to reason, Colonel Kingsley," Carpenter begged.

"Captain Carpenter, in exactly one hour I am going to sink your boat and put the torch to it," growled the Confederate officer. "Anyone or anything still on it at that time will burn with it."

By the time the *West Wind* left the Pocahontas Bar an hour later, twilight had descended. But the river was brightly illuminated by the towering flames of the *Pathfinder's* funeral pyre as she burned to the waterline where Kingsley had sunk her.

At sunset the *West Wind* anchored in midstream; there was no tying up at the bank for the night as long as the hostile Sioux stood vigil on the shore.

Chapter Ten

"Good afternoon, Captain," Rebecca said with stiff formality as she ascended the last step into the wheelhouse. She was carrying a steaming coffee cup in one hand and a plate of biscuits and beans in the other. A mewling cat followed her.

Cole turned his attention away from the river for a moment. He eyed the food but said nothing.

"This is for you," she said.

"Your thoughtfulness is touching," he said sarcastically.

"Your sentiments are wasted on me, Captain," the woman advised, setting the cup and plate on a bench. "If someone didn't bring you something to eat, you'd have to go get it yourself and we'd have to stop the boat."

She sat down and picked up the cat, which settled into her lap and began purring.

Cole looked back, puzzled at her remaining.

"Mind if I stay?" she asked coldly.

He shrugged his shoulders. "Your father's running this boat for now."

Rebecca smiled. "For now, Captain?"

He didn't respond to that. But he was hungry. He stepped back for an instant and grabbed the coffee cup, taking a sip of the hot brown fluid without looking at it. He grimaced and spit out liquid. "This isn't coffee; it's river water!" He glared at Rebecca.

"No more coffee," she said.

"We have fifty pounds of it aboard."

"Not anymore. Father felt it was breaking faith with the rest of the South to drink coffee," she explained. "You can't imagine how scarce real coffee is throughout the Confederacy. Besides, Missouri River water is supposed to be good for you."

"No thanks." He set the cup down on the bench and grabbed a biscuit. It was still doughy and only half-cooked. "What about some beef to go with it, or a duck?"

"No more cooking in the galley," Rebecca declared. "If we can't bake it or warm it by setting it atop the boilers, we don't make it. Father says we need every stick of wood for the boilers and can't waste it on cooking. You'll have to settle for beans."

Cole sighed.

"Don't complain about the food, Captain," Rebecca scolded. "The South has endured for years on smaller rations than that."

"And they'll get smaller aboard the *West Wind*," declared Cole. "We weren't provisioned for the large number of people we're carrying."

"Then it's important that you get us to Fort Benton as fast as you can."

But Cole didn't really want to reach Fort Benton; he was sure Kingsley would burn the *West Wind* then. So a slow trip would give him the chance to get the *West Wind* back. Somehow.

Cole glanced at Rebecca. "How come you didn't send someone else up with the food? Why did you come?"

"I was bored," she answered. "Came up to look at the scenery."

Cole grinned in spite of himself; he knew how she hated the bleak river landscape. He gave the wheel a slight turn. "Nobody to talk to below?"

"Just Puss here," she said, stroking the cat's fur. "He's the nicest of the bunch you brought aboard at St. Joseph."

"Mm. There were some lady passengers on the *Pathfinder*. Won't they talk to you?" He smiled wickedly.

Rebecca glared at him. "You know they won't even look at me."

"Your father?"

"Lost in thought all the time. He has much to think about."

"I'm sure. Captain Raasch?"

"We have nothing in common but our cause."

"Major Van Hill would probably talk to you."

"I can't stand the sight of a Yankee uniform, even if he weren't at the bar all the time." She rested her head against the bulkhead. "I'll be glad when the war is finally over and all the Yankee uniforms have been driven out of the South."

"Hmph. The war is over, Miss Kingsley. For everyone except Thaddius Kingsley, that is. And you."

"We will never submit to living under an oppressive Union government. There will be no compromise. We will fight on to final victory."

Cole looked at her, astonished. "You really mean that, don't you? Or is that just an excuse to load yourselves down with gold. Steal it in the name of the Confederacy, then—"

Rebecca jumped to her feet. "I resent that!" she screamed, startling Cole. The cat had dropped from her lap and dashed out the door.

"I'll bet that this so-called mission of his wasn't ordered by any higher command."

"This mission is father's own contribution to the war effort."

"Just as I thought."

"Captain Cole, my father is a noble, honorable man, without a trace of avarice or hypocrisy in him." She stepped closer to Cole. "You, Captain, have a hard time understanding any man who doesn't share your morals. Why do you think father doesn't use the other pilots in the hold? Because he knows they wouldn't think twice about the value of this boat if they thought they could stop father by wrecking it.''

"Sure, it's not their boat," he said bitterly.

She spun around and stepped to a side window.

Cole stared at her back for a moment. He softened his tone. "Miss Kingsley, neither you nor your father are facing reality. The war is lost. All you can do now is continue pointless destruction and killing.''

"Don't be absurd. My father is sick of killing.''

"Is he?" Cole asked angrily. "Look at us. We're in the middle of Dakota Territory with our fireboxes almost empty and the Sioux dogging us every inch of the way. We're overloaded with people, were carrying insufficient food, and the hold is full of miserable men trying to keep their sanity in a pitch black, stinking, filthy dungeon, all the while waiting for some sawyer or snag to smash its limbs through the hull and drown 'em all.''

"What's that smoke over there?" she asked, pointing out the window.

"Don't change the subject!''

She ignored his command. "Over there," she repeated.

He looked. "That, Miss Kingsley, is the last woodyard we stopped at. The Indians were burning it, remember?" he said angrily.

She turned to look at him. "But that was hours ago. How can we still see it?''

"It's more than fifteen miles by river, but only about two miles as the crow flies. The Missouri River has some devilish curves and loops in it.''

"I didn't realize they were that extreme." She turned to look back at the smoke column.

"Which is why the soldiers who got off the *Pathfinder* will long since have spread the word about your father. They can march cross country and cut miles off a trip between any two points on the river. You don't see the Sioux having any trouble keeping up with us just by walking, do you?''

"No, that's true."

Cole heard someone coming toward the wheelhouse from the rear. He looked back just in time to see Van Hill stumble on the few steps leading to the skylight roof. He picked himself up, brushed his hands together, and tottered forward.

"Cap'n Cole," he called boisterously from the bottom of the wheelhouse steps.

"What is it, Major?" Cole said in irritation. "You don't have to shout."

Van Hill grabbed the doorjamb with both hands and helped himself into the wheelhouse. He staggered to the forward windows. "Cap'n, this is our chance," he slurred.

"For what?"

Van Hill turned and came close to Cole, eyeing Rebecca suspiciously. "That's Fort Sully ahead," he whispered. "On the right. You gotta beach the boat now or smash her in front o' the fort."

"No," Cole refused firmly. "I'm not wrecking this boat."

Van Hill clenched his fists. "These Rebs'll go on burnin' and—"

"No, they won't," Cole said. He looked from one window to another, apparently searching for something. Finally he pointed. "There. Look over there along the shore."

"What are we supposed to see?" Rebecca asked.

"That box. See that box on the shore?"

"Yes. So?"

"That's been jettisoned by a steamboat recently."

"How do you know that?" Rebecca asked. "Might not that box have been sitting there for weeks?"

"No. The Indians watch the river closely. Anything washed up on shore gets salvaged immediately. No, that box was dumped recently."

"You mean," Rebecca said, the revelation suddenly hitting her, "that there is another steamboat ahead of us?" She peered intently out the forward window.

"Yes," Cole confirmed. "Occasionally I see her smoke. Then more cargo comes floating down the river, and the smoke disappears. She'll do anything to keep ahead of us. Anything."

"Doesn't matter," Van Hill claimed. "You gotta beach the *West Wind* anyway."

"No," Cole declared. "The longer I keep going, the better chance the men in the hold have of staying alive and of me keeping my boat."

"You're about to lose it anyway," Van Hill stated.

"Why do you say that?" Cole asked.

Van Hill pointed to the bluffs in the distance upriver. "There's a section going into battery on the hills."

"Battery?" Rebecca asked.

Van Hill pointed again. "Up there on the bluffs. Cannon."

Cole stepped hurriedly away from the wheel and grabbed the telescope from the corner of the wheelhouse. He focused on the bluffs. Two field guns, just like Kingsley's, were being unlimbered and wheeled into position on an outstretch of the bluffs. Gun crews scurried about, backing up caissons and hustling ammunition forward. Cole could make out an officer staring back at him through field glasses.

He lowered the telescope. "Uh-oh," he said simply. He swallowed hard.

Rebecca whirled and exited the wheelhouse, picked up her skirts a bit, and ran across the hurricane deck toward the stairs.

Van Hill laughed as he watched her scamper across the deck. "Now we got 'em on the run." He looked at Cole. "Those guns'll make kindling of this boat."

Cole wiped a hand across his mouth. Now what? Beach the *West Wind*? Kingsley would burn her. And shoot him. Try to run past the guns? The *West Wind* would be sunk, and the men in the hold would be drowned. And Kingsley would shoot him. And what if a cannonball hit the boilers? Everyone might be killed in the resulting explosion. And if not, Kingsley would shoot him. Cole didn't see any attractive options.

Van Hill laughed again. He lurched to the door and stuck his head out. "Come on, Colonel," he shouted, waving his arm. "Come take a look."

Cole looked over at the stairs and saw Kingsley and Raasch running across the hurricane deck toward the wheelhouse. The two men bounded up and ran to the forward window to stand next to Van Hill and stare.

"So much for your element of surprise, Colonel," Cole said.

"Captain," Kingsley asked, "where does the channel go past the bluffs?"

"More or less right down the middle of the river."

"What would you estimate the range, Captain Raasch?"

"Extreme, sir. But they've got elevation and we don't. We couldn't hit them from the boat, but they should be able to hit us."

"Kingsley," Cole said hopefully. "Surrender."

"Never," Kingsley snapped. He took a deep breath and let it out slowly. "Let's see how determined that commander is, Captain Raasch. Get all the passengers and have them line the starboard railings. Particularly the women."

"Yes, sir." Raasch quickly left the wheelhouse.

"Kingsley," Cole protested, "if that commander has as little regard for human life as you do, he'll shoot anyway. And a lot of innocent people will be killed. Not to mention yourself and your daughter, too, probably."

"If anybody is killed," Kingsley retorted, "it will be none of my doing. They are the ones who will be doing the shooting."

"But you're the one who'll be exposing the people to danger. It'll be your responsibility," argued Cole.

"What are you gonna do, Cap'n Cole?" Van Hill asked

pointedly. He was smiling with obvious pleasure at Cole's predicament.

Kingsley looked quickly at Cole. The colonel drew Cole's own pistol from his belt, cocked the hammer, and pointed it at him. "Don't get any ideas about putting this steamboat aground, Captain," he warned. "So help me, if you stop this boat or put her aground, I'll shoot you where you stand."

"He's bluffing," Van Hill said.

"I am not bluffing, Captain," Kingsley said.

Cole didn't think Kingsley was bluffing. And he was worried.

Before Cole could say anything more, Van Hill exclaimed happily, "They're firin' on us!" He laughed.

Cole and Kingsley turned and looked quickly toward the bluff. It was enveloped in a huge cloud of white smoke.

Two water spouts erupted in the channel ahead of the *West Wind* as the sharp, double crack of distant cannonfire echoed down the river.

Cole said, "Colonel, they'll destroy us. A cannonball will go right through this boat and the bottom."

"Those were warning shots," Kingsley said. "I think they're bluffing."

"What if you're wrong?" Cole asked nervously. "What if that officer is as ruthless as you are?"

Van Hill chuckled. Cole glared at him, furious.

Another cloud of smoke obscured the bluff, and another pair of geysers mushroomed ahead of the boat, close enough this time to throw water onto the forecastle. Passengers screamed and hurried aft.

"Same place as before," Cole observed. "Kingsley, you can't take us through that. It'd be murder." His hand moved tentatively for the signal bell again.

"Don't!" Kingsley pointed the pistol at Cole's face. "You keep this boat on course!"

Cole withdrew his hand, his heart pounding.

"This time'll do it," Van Hill said gleefully. "They'll hit us for sure."

"Don't sound so happy about it, Major," Cole sputtered angrily. "The next cannonball could take your head off."

"Here they come," announced Kingsley.

Cole held his breath, and he noticed that even Kingsley tensed.

Two more shot splashed into the river, but the spouts were farther ahead of the *West Wind* than the previous ones.

"Hah!" Kingsley shouted triumphantly. "You see? Their emotions have defeated military necessity."

Cole let out his breath in relief.

Van Hill was stricken. "They're not gonna hit us," he said.

"They can see the passengers," Cole said, irritated. "At least that commander cares something about people's lives."

Van Hill rushed for the door and fell down the steps, rising to run uncertainly for the edge of the hurricane deck. "Shoot!" he screamed. "Shoot!"

But no more cannonfire issued from the bluff. The gun crews merely stood at their guns and watched the *West Wind* slowly make her way up the river.

With a bowed head, Van Hill sat down heavily on the deck. He ran a hand over his hair, then let the hand fall limply across his lap. He sat there, cross-legged, as the *West Wind* steamed past Fort Sully.

"Colonel," Cole said calmly, not betraying the fear he still felt. "There's shoal water up ahead and bars. We're going to go aground soon and there's nothing I can do to avoid it."

"Very well, Captain," Kingsley answered. He seemed quite relaxed. "The fort won't give us any trouble. The passengers are still aboard whether we're aground or not." He let the hammer of the Colt down and stuck the weapon back in his belt. Cole breathed easier.

Shortly the *West Wind* lurched and slithered to a stop. Cole rang the signal bell. He leaned over the speaking tube. "Shut off the main engines, Mr. O'Brien. Let's save our steam."

Kingsley left the wheelhouse and headed for the stairs. Cole followed, but stopped next to Van Hill. The officer showed no emotion.

"Major, you act as if some terrible calamity had befallen us."

"They shoulda sunk us," Van Hill mumbled. "Spineless officers. If only I'd been there."

"A lot of people would've died," Cole pointed out.

"But the Rebs would've been stopped," Van Hill whined.

Cole stared down at the man. He realized that Van Hill and Kingsley were equally desperate in the pursuit of their respective goals.

Cole said no more. He descended to the boiler deck, avoiding the stares and mumbled apprehensions of the passengers gathered in knots there, and proceeded down to the main deck, where Moore had the spars in operation. Kingsley and Raasch were watching the action.

"Thought we'd almost had it there for a moment, Zach," Moore confided, shouting above the deafening chug of the auxiliary engines as they strained to pull the boat forward.

"Me too, Burt," Cole agreed. "Take your time sparring," he shouted closely into Moore's ear. "I want the hatch covers off as long as possible so the men in the hold can get some fresh air."

Moore nodded vigorously. "Really stinks down there, Zach."

"Colonel," Raasch said. "They're going to try to board us." He pointed toward Fort Sully.

All eyes followed his gesture. A ragged column of infantry was filing down the face of the bluff. Along the beach, several small boats were being righted and oars placed into oarlocks.

"Oh, no," Cole said.

"Captain Raasch," Kingsley ordered. "Put a shot into those troops."

"Yes, sir."

Raasch turned to his gun crew. "Right gun, train right," he ordered. He sighted down the cannon barrel as the gun was being moved. "Hold it. Prime."

Devlin, acting as gun captain, placed a small cylindrical metal fuse into the vent of the cannon, and Raasch inserted the hook of his lanyard into the fuse's pin. He stood back, then yanked the lanyard.

The cannon belched flame and smoke, and the recoil rolled the weapon backward.

On the beach, soldiers crouched or dropped to the ground. But the iron shot bounced harmlessly on the dirt and quickly rolled dead. The officers exhorted their men to action, but the blue-coated soldiers were reluctant to go to the boats.

"Captain Raasch," Kingsley said. "It seems those Yankee officers need more of a warning. Give 'em a round of canister."

"Yes, sir, but it's too far for canister."

"That's okay," Kingsley said. "Just let them know what they'd be rowing into."

The gun was sponged and a linen cartridge of powder was shoved down its throat and rammed home. A round of canister, a loosely constructed can containing twenty-seven small iron balls, was thrust into the muzzle and rammed home. The gun crew waited, standing aside.

"Prime." Devlin put another fuse in place. Raasch inserted his lanyard, stretched it out and fired the gun. The projectiles fanned out and spattered the river with a deadly rain.

None of the balls reached the shore, but the effect on the troops on the beach was marked. All activity at the boats ceased. Even the officers were motionless now.

Kingsley glanced at Cole with a grin on his face. "A wise commander," he said.

Raasch had the gun reloaded with canister.

"Colonel!" A soldier came running forward on the main deck. "Colonel, the roustabouts are tryin' to escape," he said, pointing astern.

Kingsley rushed to the side of the boat and climbed the starboard bull rails to look back.

Cole, alarmed, did likewise.

Like a black trickle of oil, the roustabouts, taking advantage of the distraction and the noise of the sparring operation, had been slipping off the starboard outrigger that flanked the sternwheel. They formed a wavy line curving away from the *West Wind* back toward Fort Sully, each man trying to wade or swim as fast as he could through the resisting medium.

"Captain Raasch, fire a warning shot over their heads," Kingsley shouted angrily. "I want them back."

"Yes, sir." Raasch turned to his men. "Train right." The gun was moved and Raasch attached his lanyard to a new fuse. Devlin reached for the elevating screw, but Raasch knocked his hand away.

"We're loaded with canister, Captain Raasch," Devlin noted. "We need more elevation or we'll hit—"

Raasch yanked the lanyard, and the blast of canister sprayed over the water. The iron balls tore a gaping hole in the line of roustabouts. Some of the Negroes spun and reeled, others pitched forward.

Devlin glared at Raasch. "You didn't have to do that."

Cole looked aghast at the black bodies bobbing on the water. "Raasch!" he screamed. He leaped the few steps to the field gun and smashed a fist into the Confederate officer's face.

Raasch crashed to the deck. Still on his back, he yanked his pistol from its holster, cocked it, and pointed it at Cole. "No Yankee touches me and lives," he snarled.

Raasch squeezed the trigger, but Devlin's foot shot out and kicked his gun hand as the pistol fired. A bullet whizzed past Cole's head and he staggered back a step.

Raasch glared at Devlin. "What do you mean by striking an officer?" he demanded angrily.

"We need Captain Cole, sir," Devlin explained.

Raasch leaped to his feet. "I'll decide if we—"

"No!" Kingsley shouted. He rushed up to the two men. "I will decide who is needed around here, Captain Raasch."

"Yes, sir," Raasch acknowledged quickly but belligerently.

Kingsley turned to Devlin. "Sergeant Devlin, it is a serious offense to strike an officer, and by rights you ought to be punished."

"Yes, sir."

"But in this case I believe your action was warranted. We do need Captain Cole too much to kill him for what he did just now."

"Sir," Raasch protested. "That Yankee struck an officer in the Confederate States Army."

"Well, I felt like doing it myself, Captain Raasch," Kingsley said angrily. "I told you to fire a warning shot, not slaughter those men. They're of no use to me dead."

Raasch was sullen but silent.

"Back to your duties, both of you."

Raasch and Devlin moved apart, and Raasch maneuvered past Cole. "I'll get you later," Raasch hissed, loud enough for only Cole to hear. "Before I leave this boat, you're a dead man."

Kingsley turned to Cole before the latter could reply to Raasch. "And as for you, Captain, do not stretch your luck too far. Now get back to the wheelhouse."

Cole nodded again. "All right."

He headed for the stairs, only to find Josh standing with his back to the boilers, drying out his wet clothes. The roustabout's face was twisted in anguish.

"Josh," Cole said, speaking as low as the auxiliary engines would permit, "what got into you roosters?"

"Cap'n, the men been slaves before, and we don' intend

to be slaves again. Ever since that colonel took over the *Wes' Wind*, we been lookin' for a chance to 'scape.''

''Well, don't try anything stupid like that again.''

Josh shuddered at the recollection of the iron balls splattering into the bodies ahead of him in line. ''No, suh!''

On the boiler deck, Cole found Rebecca at the side railing, staring astern at the black bodies, now only small dots, floating face down in the muddy brown water. Cole walked up to her.

''Pretty, isn't it?'' he commented coldly. ''First the Indians at that village and now my roosters.''

Rebecca turned slowly to face him. Her brow was furrowed. ''It's—'' She stopped to clear her throat. ''It's war.''

''Right. It's war,'' Cole repeated with disgust. He turned and headed for the stairs to the hurricane deck.

Chapter Eleven

That night Cole lay awake long after the *West Wind* had anchored in the middle of the river. The wound in his side was healing properly, but it bothered him constantly. And the physical discomfort was a steady reminder of the danger he was in. He lay on his bunk and stared blankly into space, trying desperately to think of a solution to his predicament.

He stiffened to alertness for a moment when he heard Raasch talking quietly to Rebecca on the boiler deck promenade.

Cole had not realized that Rebecca was still up and walking the decks. His ears easily picked up the conversation outside.

"You're up very late, Miss Kingsley," Raasch said. "Somethin' bothering you?"

She didn't answer.

"Moonlight becomes you, Miss Kingsley," Raasch went on smoothly.

Still she didn't answer.

"Haven't seen you lookin' purtier. It's a shame you don't smile once in awhile."

Rebecca said quietly but firmly, "I do not appreciate your attentions, Captain Raasch."

"As an officer and a gentleman," Raasch snapped, "I resent your attitude that—"

"The Army can make you an officer, Captain Raasch," Rebecca shot out, "but there's little they can do about making you a gentleman."

Cole heard Raasch's foot clunk off the bottom plate of the railing.

"And you wouldn't even be an officer," Rebecca went on, "if the Army weren't so short of men."

"I won't take that kind of talk even from you," Raasch snarled.

Cole raised his eyebrows. Carefully he swung his bootless feet off the bunk and sat up, wincing briefly at the stab of pain in his side. He padded quietly over to the closed cabin door and leaned closer to listen more carefully.

"And if you weren't an officer," Rebecca said, "those roustabouts would still be alive."

"They tried to run."

"You still think like an overseer," she accused. "The worst thing this war has done is to give the likes of you a false respectability."

"You pious little snip," Raasch snarled. "I've given four years of my life to the Confederacy."

"I'll give you credit for that, Captain," Rebecca allowed.

"Maybe I'd like more than just credit from you, little Miss Stuck-up," Raasch said.

"Take your hands off me, Captain Raasch," Cole heard Rebecca say sharply.

Without even thinking, Cole whipped open the cabin door. He casually stepped outside and stopped. "Good evening, Miss Kingsley, Captain Raasch," he said.

Raasch let go of Rebecca's arm. He glared at Cole. "We didn't ask you out here," he said.

"I invited myself," Cole said. "It's my boat."

"Not anymore it ain't," Raasch said. He took a step toward Cole.

Rebecca said, "I don't think my father would appreciate you two getting into a fight, Captain Raasch."

Raasch stopped and looked back at her. He glared at her for a moment, then said, "We'll have another talk some other time, Miss Stuck-up." Then he stomped past Cole and disappeared around the corner of the superstructure.

Rebecca nodded to Cole. "Thank you, Captain. Your appearance was most timely."

Cole bowed. "Happy to be of service, Miss Kingsley."

Rebecca turned to the railing. She folded her arms and rested her head against a stanchion.

Cole felt drawn to her. He started forward cautiously. She didn't seem to mind his approach, but he had to admit it seemed more like cold indifference than welcome.

Joining her at the railing he stared at the dimly visible prairie that stretched from the shore of the Missouri to the everpresent, monotonous brown bluffs farther back. When he squinted he could just make out the shapes of the nightly watch of the Sioux, squatting on the bluffs, always watching, always waiting.

"They're still there, aren't they?" Rebecca said, looking at Cole and noticing his squint.

He could see that her brow was furrowed. "Yes," he said softly, "they're still there."

"And after all these miles," she commented. She looked back at the bluffs. "I have to admire their spirit, if not their cause."

"Not their cause?" Cole asked. "Raasch murdered innocent men, women, and children at that Indian village. Seems you and the Sioux are much alike."

Her head spun around. "I beg your pardon," she said angrily.

"They're following us because their families were murdered. You're on this boat because your mother was killed."

"But . . ."

Cole waited, but she didn't finish her sentence. Finally she turned back to stare at the bluffs.

He gazed at her profile. He could no longer see the fierce determination and confidence that he had seen there for so many days. She had seemed as hard as boiler iron, but now . . .

"Raasch was right, you know," he said finally. "About you having too pretty a face to ruin by not smiling at least once in awhile."

She showed no change in expression or emotion. She didn't even look at Cole. Finally she said, "Four years ago I could have spent a delightful evening of coquettish flirtation with you, Captain. Now flirting seems so—silly."

Cole straightened up and took a short step back. "I meant no offense, Miss Kingsley."

She continued to stare out over the water.

Cole studied her features. The moonlight softened the lines of her tense face, put a glow in her cheeks, and even a twinkle in her eye. "Miss Kingsley, I would like to say that I admire your spirit, if not your cause."

She made no response, and Cole quietly turned and padded back toward his cabin.

"Captain," she called as he was about to disappear inside.

He stopped and looked back at her. "Yes?"

"Thank you," she said. And she smiled at him.

He smiled back. "You're welcome, Miss Kingsley."

Chapter Twelve

The *West Wind* overtook the steamboat *Big Horn* the next day, squatting in the mud in the eddy of a crossing. Captain Stevens was distraught when Raasch brought him aboard the *West Wind*.

"I was hoping we'd never overtake you, Elias," a chagrinned Cole said. "What happened?"

"Rudders," the disgusted captain said with a shake of his head. "Lost the first one going over a bar four days ago. Didn't have time to replace it; you were too close. A sawyer clipped off the other one yesterday. I drifted into that bar yonder before I could get my anchors set. I've almost got a new rudder made, and another couple of hours would've seen me off and running again." Stevens was bitter.

"I'm sorry," Cole said. "The colonel's revolver is a pretty good persuader for speed on my part."

Kingsley interrupted, leafing through some manifests. "I'll have to confiscate some of your provisions, Captain Stevens, but Captain Raasch tells me you've already jettisoned most of your cargo."

"That's right. Trying to stay ahead of you bandits."

Kingsley stiffened and looked harshly at the steamboat captain. "We are not bandits, sir," he declared. "We are soldiers in the Confederate States Army."

"Bah!" Stevens retorted. "There's no Confederacy left, so you can't use that as an excuse for your thieving anymore."

"Are there not still Confederate armies in the field?" Kingsley argued. "Has the government of the Confederacy been taken into custody?"

"Oh, a few ragtag outfits still fighting, I guess. And ol' Jeff Davis hasn't been found yet, but he will be. And probably be strung up on the spot. I hear the Union Army's just achin' to lynch him ever since Abe was shot."

"Lincoln shot?" Cole sputtered.

"What?" Kingsley gasped. "Dead?"

"Sure. Didn't you know? Happened almost two weeks ago. A guy named Booth shot him while he was watchin' a play."

"No!"

"Well," a sobered Kingsley said, "can't say I feel sorry for the tyrant, but it was a mistake to assassinate him. That'll only make a martyr of him." The colonel sighed. "Anyway, we will take most of your wood, too. And all valuables in your strongbox and in possession of your passengers and crew will be confiscated and transferred to the *West Wind*. You will make preparations to receive on board your vessel all passengers now on this one."

"How's that?" Stevens said, startled. Cole looked quickly at Kingsley.

"In addition to the passengers, you will take aboard most of the crew of the *Pathfinder*, the decksweep of the *West Wind*, the chambermaids, waiters, cooks, and so forth. I need only a few roustabouts. Oh, and take Major Van Hill with you. The man's a drunken nuisance and a disgrace to any country's uniform."

Stevens' face brightened. "You're not going to burn my boat?" he asked hopefully.

"No. We couldn't possibly hold all your passengers and crew in addition to those already aboard the *West Wind*. And our food supply is running low. I will retain only Captain Carpenter and Mr. Kellogg. They will stay in the hold to ensure Captain Cole's cooperation. But first, Captain

Stevens, I will have you sign a bond of ransom for the boat, payable upon the end of hostilities.''

Stevens winked at Cole. ''Be happy to sign your bond, Colonel.''

''And, Captain Stevens, since wood is so difficult to obtain, I want you to turn around and head back downriver. We need all the wood for ourselves.''

''Whatever you say, Colonel.''

''All right. Be off with you.''

''Yes, sir, Colonel.''

Raasch had the captain rowed back to the *Big Horn*, and the transfer of wood, valuables, and people began at once.

The river was already filled with the shaggy heads of swimming buffalo, but more were pouring down the bluffs from the east, milling about in a giant herd on the prairie, and then plunging into the river. And on the other side, the shore and bluffs were black with the creatures heading west.

Cole stopped the *West Wind* and ordered the anchors put out. He stepped to the forward window of the wheelhouse to watch in awe the vast multitude of huge animals filling his view of the river. Kingsley came clumping up the stairs to the hurricane deck and stomped into the wheelhouse.

''Captain Cole, why have you stopped the boat?''

''We can't steam through that herd of buffalo, Colonel.''

''Why not?'' the Confederate officer asked, exasperated. He stepped to the front window. ''They'll move out of the way.''

''No, they won't,'' Cole corrected him. ''Buffalo won't change course for anybody or anything.''

''Well, so what? Just run right over them.''

''Colonel, their heads are like iron. An angry bull could punch a hole in our hull and sink us.''

''That herd could take all day to pass,'' Kingsley said. ''I'll take the risk of a sinking.''

"The men in the hold might feel differently, Colonel," Cole said earnestly.

Kingsley faced him. "Captain, I am going to move the *West Wind* immediately. Would you like the men in the hold to take their chances on me piloting this boat or on you."

Cole was sure Kingsley meant what he said. Every time they heard of another Confederate disaster, the colonel got more desperate in his haste.

"All right, Colonel," Cole said.

Kingsley turned back to the window. Cole took the wheel and reached over and rang the signal bell. "Mr. O'Brien," he called into the speaking tube. "Tell Mr. Moore to weigh anchor."

Shortly the *West Wind* began moving again. He rang for slow and tried to find a gap, but there was simply no open water anywhere in the wall of brown heads ahead of him. Cole sent the *West Wind* straight into the herd. He was sure that those in the hold could hear heads clunking against the wooden sides of the steamboat's hull.

Cole turned the wheel to correct course, and then turned it even more. The *West Wind* didn't respond. The steam engine started blowing off excess steam.

"What's wrong?" Kingsley asked anxiously.

"She's not responding," Cole said. "And O'Brien just stopped the engines."

Both men looked aft; the sternwheel was motionless.

"Why have the engines stopped?"

Cole pointed aft. "Here comes Josh. O'Brien must've sent him."

Josh bounded up the steps to the wheelhouse. "Cap'n, Mistah Brien said to tell you one o' them buff'lo done stuck hisself in the sternwheel."

Cole glanced at Kingsley with some satisfaction. "I told you there'd be trouble."

"Then you'd better get us out of it," Kingsley snapped.

Without retorting Cole shouted into the speaking tube.

"O'Brien, tell Mr. Moore to set the anchors immediately. We mustn't drift."

Cole turned to Josh. "Go see what you can do about getting that bull out of the sternwheel, Josh. Fast!"

"Yes, suh!" Josh leaped out of the wheelhouse and raced for the stairs.

"We're drifting," Kingsley said.

Cole glanced astern. "If we don't get an anchor set right away, we'll drift smack into that bar with the driftwood."

Moore was quick with the anchors, but the muddy bottom didn't give immediate purchase, and the anchors dragged. The steamboat drifted sternfirst into the bar, smashing into some tree trunks and limbs that had washed up there. The boat sagged to a halt.

Cole smirked at Kingsley. "Well, Colonel?"

"Captain, we shall take a look at the problem close up," Kingsley said. "Follow me."

Cole shook his head. Kingsley would never admit he'd made a mistake. He followed Kingsley down the stairs and descended all the way to the main deck. They joined O'Brien, who was standing on an outrigger and looking at the buffalo which had stopped the *West Wind's* sternwheel. Several soldiers were crammed onto the other outrigger to stare at the wounded buffalo. Cole and Kingsley joined O'Brien.

"Looks bad, Captain," O'Brien reported. "This here bull's got himself jammed in real good, and he's smashed two of the buckets."

The buffalo was squeezed between the end of the sternwheel's paddle arms and the cylinder timber. Most of the time he lay limp, panting heavily, eyes bulging, blood flowing from his nostrils and mouth. Then he would burst into frenzied action, trying to free himself from the machinery in which he was entangled.

"Not only that," O'Brien continued, "but he's bent the clamp on the pillow block, and the connecting rod's twisted and come loose."

The bull bellowed and banged his head against the paddle arm. "Well, you want to wait until he tears the whole sternwheel apart?" Cole barked. "Shoot him."

Kingsley nodded to the soldiers on the other outrigger. One of them raised his musket, cocked the hammer, aimed at the forehead of the shaggy animal, and fired.

The buffalo roared and lunged, hooves rattling against the wood, and his head, gushing blood down his snout, banged against the paddle arm again. The board cracked.

"Shoot him again!" Cole shouted.

Another soldier drew a bead on the animal from just three feet away and fired. The bull flinched, then stopped thrashing.

"Magnificent creature," Kingsley said. "Just wouldn't die."

Just like some Confederates, Cole thought to himself.

"Captain," O'Brien said. He was squatting and looking down into the water under the stern. "It's worse than I thought. One of the rudders is missing." ·

Cole snorted. "We must be sitting on it."

"And the other's twisted on the stern post. Looks like the trees mashed us good."

Kingsley was looking into the water, too. He was frowning. "How long do you estimate for repairs?"

The engineer stood up. "A day, maybe two."

Cole was pleased; with the *West Wind* stuck, they couldn't overtake any other boats.

Kingsley looked at Cole. Cole wanted to gloat, but Kingsley didn't give him the chance.

"Fix it," Kingsley said simply. Then he turned and strode angrily off the outrigger, shoving a soldier out of his way.

Two days later, the *West Wind's* steam was back up. The sternwheel thrashed and the auxiliary engines whined and chugged. The spars creaked and groaned and the steamboat finally pulled itself free of the bar. On the forecastle deck, Moore had the spars hoisted inboard immediately and secured.

Cole steered the *West Wind* back into the channel and settled in to another long stand at the wheel, but Kingsley and Raasch mounted the stairs from the boiler deck and marched over to the wheelhouse.

"Fortune smiles upon our enterprise, Captain," Kingsley said with a grin as he mounted the wheelhouse steps. "I was afraid we'd see no more steamboats, but here comes one to the party through the back door."

Cole jerked his head around and stiffened, seeing a twin column of smoke downriver. "Another boat," he said forlornly. "Stupid fool."

Kingsley found the boat's telescope and lifted it to his eye. "Captain Cole, anchor the boat. We'll wait for her to catch up." The two Confederates left the wheelhouse.

Reluctantly, Cole rang the signal bell. "Mr. O'Brien," he called down through the speaking tube. "Have Mr. Moore set the anchors. Then stop the engines."

Once the *West Wind* was securely anchored, Cole left the wheelhouse and joined Kingsley and Raasch, who were standing at the after end of the hurricane deck, taking turns with the telescope.

"This is almost too easy, Captain Cole," Kingsley commented. He was smiling.

Cole said nothing. He only stared despondently at the two columns of smoke, now grown larger. From the looks of it, the steamboat was putting all she had into her run. Probably had the safety valves tied down, racing to her own destruction, Cole thought.

The image of the other steamboat, far down the river, grew larger. Cole could make out the big smokestacks, the deck configuration, and her high wheelhouse. He wished her captain would recognize the *West Wind*—her name was plainly visible on the after bulkhead of the wheelhouse—

and turn around. But thick black smoke kept pouring from the other boat's smokestacks, and the bow wave rose high on her hull.

Cole frowned. He thought the boat looked familiar, but there was something odd about all that cargo stacked on her forecastle deck. "Colonel, may I have that telescope a minute?"

Kingsley handed Cole the telescope.

Cole peered through the tubes, then lowered the telescope and frowned. "I don't understand it," he said finally, "but that's the *Big Horn* again."

"Coming back upriver?" Kingsley asked. He took the telescope away from Cole and squinted through the instrument himself. "Why, they've built breastwork on both decks on the front of the boat. Not only breastwork, but embrasures for cannon."

"Cannon?" Cole said in alarm.

"The two from Fort Sully," Raasch said.

"No doubt," Kingsley agreed. "They must've dropped down as far as the fort, dumped their passengers, armed the boat with the cannon and bluecoats, and—" He paused while he examined the image of the boat. "Well, well, well. If it isn't Major Van Hill. The man's got more fight in him than I thought."

"Oh, no," Cole mumbled with apprehension. "I can't believe this."

"Shall we turn and attack, sir?" Raasch asked.

"Attack?" Cole exclaimed. "A cannon battle between steamboats? Kingsley, solid shot will go through these bulkheads like they were paper. A shot in a boiler will—"

"He will be taking the same risks that we are, Captain," Kingsley argued. "Still, a battle like this does entail risk to our mission." He looked at Cole. "Do you think you can outrun that boat for awhile?"

"I'll sure try," Cole promised. "But only until we hit the first sandbar."

"Yes, but it will give me some time to bring my guns to bear on the *Big Horn*. A few shots may convince those bluecoats that it was safer back at Fort Sully, and that may be the end of it. All right, get going. We haven't a minute to lose. The *Big Horn* will soon be in range."

"I'm on my way!" Cole turned and ran for the wheel-house.

"Captain Raasch," Kingsley said. "Move the guns to the boiler deck. Cut holes in that partition at the stern for gun ports." The after end of the *West Wind's* boiler deck was finished off by a high bulkhead against which were constructed the laundry facilities and the two toilets, extending slightly over the sternwheel. A short section on each end of the bulkhead had no covering structures, and it was to these two places that Kingsley was pointing. "We'll engage the enemy as soon as he's within range."

"Yes, sir."

Cole took the steps into the wheelhouse in just two bounds. Frantically he rang the signal bell. "Sam, gimme all the steam you can!" he yelled into the speaking tube. "Tell Moore to weigh anchor immediately."

Cole waited impatiently. Finally he heard the engines start chugging and the sternwheel burst into motion.

A geyser erupted to the right of the *West Wind's* bow. Cringing, Cole looked back just in time to see a solid shot slam into the spinning sternwheel and throw chunks of several buckets into the air. Cole heard the crack and rumble of the distant cannonfire from the *Big Horn*.

He gripped the wheel tightly. The *West Wind* could not outrun cannonballs.

Chapter Thirteen

As the *West Wind* struggled to make headway, another salvo of twelve-pound balls found her. Cole flinched as each shot hit the *West Wind*, the first one punching a hole in the hurricane deck near the edge and tearing off a section of boiler deck railing before plunging into the water.

The second shot smashed through the stern bulkhead where Kingsley's men were working. A Rebel soldier dropped to his knees, cursing and pulled a huge, jagged splinter from his bleeding arm. Two men rushed to help him, but the others continued chopping embrasures in the bulkhead or struggling with the field guns, trying to get them moved into position. When the Confederates had gotten their two field guns positioned at the after bulkhead ammunition was brought up and the two guns loaded.

Two more shots came hurtling toward the *West Wind*, both penetrating deep inside the steamboat. One ripped through three cabins and dislodged the galley stove. The other iron ball crashed through both hurricane and boiler decks and killed a roustabout in the engine room.

Cole jumped when Kingsley's two guns finally answered the *Big Horn* with their own blasts of fire and smoke. The guns recoiled on the sloping deck of the *West Wind* and rolled back to clunk against the cabin superstructure with no breechings to stop the roll.

Cole screamed into the speaking tube again. "More speed, O'Brien!" He didn't want his boat destroyed by

117

cannonfire, and he didn't want Kingsley killing anyone on
the *Big Horn* either.

Kingsley's guns were reloaded and rolled back to poke
their muzzles through the improvised gun ports. They fired
again and Cole turned to watch the effect. He cringed at
the marksmanship of the Rebel artillerymen. Both shots hit
the *Big Horn*. Cole saw wood fly into the air, and he
clenched his teeth at the thought of the shot and splinters
hitting men. But the *Big Horn* kept coming.

The *West Wind's* sternwheel was hit again, and more men
were wounded on the main deck as the shot continued
through the thin bulkhead. A shot smashed the men's toilet,
and a piece of a door skewered a man at Kingsley's starboard
gun and killed him instantly.

At the next salvo a forward corner post of the wheelhouse
was torn off with half the forward bulkhead. Every pane of
glass in the wheelhouse shattered, and glass sprayed over
the interior of the wheelhouse, as well as over Cole.

The captain threw up an arm to shield his face from the
flying shards. This is insanity, he thought. The *Big Horn's*
guns were already pulverizing the *West Wind* at long distance, but the steamboat would slow as her sternwheel was
broken up. The *Big Horn* would eventually overtake the
West Wind and would blaze away at her at point blank range.

Kingsley's two field guns spoke again, but there was an
immediate response from the *Big Horn*. More pieces of the
sternwheel flew up. A shot landed on the muzzle of the
starboard field gun, dismounted it, and blasted fragments
of the barrel into the gun crew, killing and wounding.

Cole yelled into the speaking tube. ''O'Brien, we've gotta
have more steam! Tie down the safety valves. More wood!''

The Confederates hastily dragged the dead against the
outside of the cabin superstructure. The wounded were carried inside the salon, though that was of dubious protection.

More cannonfire came. More crashing and splintering of

wood, more cries of agony, more slipping on the blood-splotched deck.

Cole turned the wheel to avoid a sawyer, but the boat did not answer the helm well; the sternwheel had been so badly damaged that the *West Wind* was making little headway. With growing apprehension, he watched the hull of the *West Wind* crunch into the tips of the limbs of the seesawing sunken tree and ride over it.

The boat slowed considerably. Then Cole heard the engines stop and blow off steam. The *West Wind* began to pay her head around as the current took control.

Cole turned the wheel first one way and then the other but with no effect. He jerked his head around and saw Kingsley and some of his men crowded around the gun ports, peering down. The sternwheel was no longer turning. The steamboat began drifting backwards.

Cole's scalp cringed. He took the steps in a single leap and hit the hurricane deck on the run, just barely halting at the edge. "Kingsley, what happened?" he yelled down to the Confederate on the boiler deck below him.

Kingsley turned. "A shot broke off one of the boards, and it's jammed the wheel."

The *West Wind* was now slowly turning athwart the channel; Kingsley's one remaining gun would no longer bear on the *Big Horn*. "Kingsley, you've got to surrender," Cole shouted down. "We'll be at the mercy of the guns on the *Big Horn*."

"Never!" Kingsley shouted. He turned to the men. "A volunteer! Someone to get that wheel turning again." Kingsley picked up one of the axes they had used to chop the gunports. "A few chops and that board will snap," he said.

Cole was astonished to see every men within six feet reach for the axe without hesitation. The outrigger was in plain field of fire from the *Big Horn*. He couldn't understand such bravery.

"I'll go," several men shouted.

Kingsley handed the axe to one of them. "Good man, soldier," he said.

The soldier ran for the forward stairs, descending to the main deck and running aft out onto the outrigger. There he started chopping at the broken bucket.

Riflefire broke out on the *Big Horn*, and minié balls started spattering the water and peppering the stern of the *West Wind*. The Big *Horn's* field guns fired again, too, but instead of two solid shots, the *West Wind* was swept with a hail of canister.

Bullets and the iron canister balls rattled against the stern and starboard sides of the *West Wind*. Cole dropped to the deck.

"Let's get this gun moved," Kingsley shouted. "Grab those wheels!"

The men manhandled the field gun around to the side of the deck. They managed to get off only one shot before minié balls and another charge of canister decimated the gun crew.

Cole hugged the hurricane deck. He was astonished to hear the soldier on the outrigger still chopping. It was incredible that all those bullets and canister had missed him.

The broken bucket finally snapped in two and fell away and the sternwheel sprang into action again.

Cole leaped to his feet and ran for the wheelhouse. Another load of canister ripped savagely into the after half of the steamboat, and one of the iron balls found the soldier on the outrigger. It slammed him against a supporting brace and he fell to the outrigger deck before dropping the axe and falling into the water.

Cole grabbed the slowly revolving wheel and spun it. The *West Wind* responded, and he turned her stern to the *Big Horn*. Kingsley's field gun was maneuvered back into position, and it banged away at the pursuing boat.

The *Big Horn* shifted back to shot. A solid shot smashed into the after bulkhead and sprayed the gun crew with razor-sharp slivers. The second shot hit the starboard smokestack and the top twenty feet of the black cylinder folded over in slow motion and crashed to the hurricane deck. The soot that had accumulated over many years of steady burning shook loose and exploded from the smokestack in a massive cloud that obscured Cole's view of the river ahead.

Suddenly Devlin bolted into the wheelhouse. "Cole, the colonel says it's no use tryin' to outrun the *Big Horn*. We're gonna turn and attack."

"It'll be the death of all of us," Cole shouted.

"Turn this boat around," Devlin ordered, "and aim straight for the *Big Horn*. We're gonna board her."

"Sergeant, if we turn our bows toward the *Big Horn*, we'll expose our boilers. The breastwork you built can't withstand solid shot. We'll be blown sky-high."

"Turn the boat, Cole!" Devlin shouted. He drove the butt of his musket into Cole's stomach and the captain crumpled and fell to the floor. Devlin grabbed the wheel and pulled it hard over with one hand. The steamboat started turning then, showing her side to the *Big Horn*.

The two cannon on the pursuing steamboat boomed eagerly at the new and larger target. They couldn't miss; the *West Wind* shuddered as the solid shot smashed into her. One shot landed in the ash pit under the boilers and sent a cloud of gritty ash dust into the faces of the fire gang and some of Kingsley's men gathered nearby. The roustabouts abandoned the fireboxes and scattered to other parts of the boat despite shouted threats; they knew what the first shot into the boilers would do. Kingsley's disciplined soldiers, however, stayed at their posts.

On the wheelhouse deck, Cole gasped for breath. He was scared. Scared and despondent. His precious boat, already shot full of gaping holes, was about to be destroyed. And when the boilers exploded, the things sailing highest through the air would be the wheelhouse and the bodies of Devlin and himself. He didn't know whom he hated more at the moment, Kingsley or Van Hill.

He could think of only one chance. If the *West Wind* were helpless and at the mercy of the *Big Horn* without a chance to fight back, even Kingsley might decide to call it quits. Even he must have some concern for the lives of his men—or at least that of his daughter.

Cole reached over and picked up a shard of glass. He leaped to his feet, grabbed Devlin around the neck from behind, and jabbed the sharp edge of the glass against the man's throat.

"Move and I cut your throat, Devlin," Cole warned.

Devlin froze.

"Drop the rifle," Cole ordered.

The rifle clattered to the deck.

With a quick thrust Cole yanked the sergeant off balance and hurled him out through the wheelhouse door. Devlin stumbled backward down the few steps he managed to touch and landed flat on his back, striking his head on the deck.

Cole lunged for the rifle, cocked it as he raised it, and pointed it at Devlin. But the sergeant didn't move. He just lay where he had landed. Cole lowered the rifle.

He turned his attention back to the *West Wind*. She had now turned downstream; the two steamboats were rushing toward each other. Cole grabbed the wheel and turned the boat again, this time pointing it toward the shore.

Cole knew that Kingsley's wrath would soon find its way up to the wheelhouse, and he waited only long enough to be sure the *West Wind* would go aground, bows on to the shore. Holding onto Devlin's rifle, he jumped from the wheelhouse and started across the hurricane deck.

The *Big Horn* fired once more and Cole heard both shots crash through bulkheads on the main deck.

Cole rushed down the stairs to the boiler deck and turned for the nearest cabin door.

"Cole!"

He whirled to see Kingsley and two soldiers at the far corner of the cabin superstructure. All three were raising rifles, Kingsley with Cole's Henry in his hands.

Cole swung the barrel of his rifle up and fired blindly. One of the soldiers staggered backward, gripping his arm. The other two men fired, but Cole hurled himself through a cabin door splintering the wood as the lockset ripped off part of the doorjamb. Both shots missed.

Cole rushed to the inside cabin door, then stepped into the salon. As he did, the *West Wind* lurched to a halt, driven onto the muddy shore.

The salon was a shambles. Broken planking and jagged beams protruded in many places, blue sky showed through much of the roof, and cabins were smashed open, with whole bulkheads knocked down and doors shattered. The entire salon was filled with broken furniture and debris.

Cole saw Rebecca helping a man toward the line of wounded lying on the deck. Her clothes were torn and dirty, her face was smudged and streaked with red where she had wiped a bloody hand across her forehead, and small slivers of wood nestled in her disheveled hair. Her eyes looked tired, her face was pallid, and she struggled wearily at the heavy weight of the man leaning on her.

Through a large hole in the cabin across from him, Cole saw the *Big Horn*, very close, charging bows on. Heavy riflefire was exchanged between the two boats and Cole could hear the angry smack of the heavy lead minié balls striking the *West Wind*. The *Big Horn's* two cannon fired again.

Cole could actually see the two iron shots hurtling straight toward him in their flight. One took off the door of a cabin and demolished what was left of the salon bar. The other crashed through a cabin bulkhead across from Rebecca and hit the wounded man she was supporting full in the chest, ripping him from her arms and knocking her down. The man landed against the far bulkhead with his torso smashed open.

Cole blanched and held a hand to his stomach. Rebecca fell to her knees. She stared wide-eyed at the dead man, her hands covering the lower part of her face, her body rocking gently back and forth, and a pitiful moan escaping her throat.

Cole ran to her, but she simply continued to rock and whimper.

"Cole!" Kingsley shouted from the forward exit of the salon.

For a dangerous moment Cole had forgotten why he had ducked into the salon. He whirled to see Kingsley taking aim again. But Cole hadn't taken any more cartridges from Devlin; the man's rifle was useless.

"Stand away from my daughter, Cole," Kingsley shouted.

Cole leaped aside. Kingsley fired, but the bullet tore into Cole's coat without hitting him. As Kingsley levered another cartridge into the rifle's chamber, Cole ran through a cabin and exited onto the boiler deck promenade.

There he stopped, confronted by the *Big Horn* about to ram the *West Wind* amidships. Blue-coated soldiers were bunched up on the guards, ready to board. Some were firing at Rebels on the *West Wind*, and the gunners at the field guns held their lanyards taut, ready for one last salvo. At the rear of the Union troops stood Major Van Hill, a pistol in one hand and a sword in the other. Cole was sickened by the triumphant look in the man's eyes.

"Cole!"

Cole turned resignedly toward Kingsley's familiar voice, but didn't try to move. Suddenly it all seemed so futile. Even if Kingsley didn't put a bullet in his chest, it would be a miracle if the two boats weren't blown up when the *Big Horn's* guns fired into the *West Wind's* boilers. Nobody on the other boat seemed to have any idea of the danger.

The loudest explosion Cole had ever heard roared in his ears, and a mighty blast of searing steam slammed him against the superstructure bulkhead. He and the *West Wind* were barraged with wood debris, pieces of boiler iron, brick, and metal that whistled and clattered like shrapnel.

With his hands over his head, Cole waited for the deadly rain to stop falling, then pressed his hands and body against the deck to try to stop the spinning sensation. Fighting the distraction of the violent ringing in his ears, he looked over at the *Big Horn*.

Her smokestacks lay in the river. The forward sections of her boiler deck and hurricane deck, along with the wheel-house, were all gone, peeled back and ripped off by the explosion of the *Big Horn's* boilers. All the breastwork, cannon, and boiler, had been blown off the steamboat. The water around her was filled with debris and bodies, and fire was spreading over the forward half of the boat.

Had Kingsley's men managed to turn their gun around and fire into the *Big Horn*? Or had the *Big Horn's* boilers finally ruptured under the extreme pressure? Cole couldn't remember.

He looked over at Kingsley. The colonel was slowly getting to his feet, with the Henry still in his grasp. He took the few steps to the railing and stood there. He didn't look at Cole, only stared at what had been a steamboat until a few seconds before.

Chapter Fourteen

Cole sensed he had nothing to fear from Kingsley and stepped to the railing himself. The anger in him at the carnage continued to rise.

"Captain Raasch?" Kingsley called.

Raasch appeared from under the overhang. "Sir?"

"See to putting out that fire as quickly as possible. Gather in any survivors from the *Big Horn* and see if you can scavenge either of the *Big Horn's* guns from the water. And transfer all of her provisions to the *West Wind*."

"Yes, sir."

Angrily, Cole strode up to Kingsley. He had a blistering lecture prepared in his mind, but Kingsley spoke first. "Can we tow that hulk if the fire is put out?"

Cole, distracted, frowned. "Why?"

"My desire to burn the *Pathfinder* blinded me to the more useful expedient of feeding the steamboat plank by plank into the *West Wind's* fireboxes. I won't make that mistake with the *Big Horn*."

Kingsley turned and headed quickly for the door to the salon. Cole called after him, but Kingsley ignored him.

Cole continued to glare at Kingsley as Moore entered the salon. "The man said nothing about the dead, Burt," Cole said.

"I was wonderin' whether you had made it," the first mate returned.

Cole clapped him on the shoulder. "Glad to see you came

through all right, Burt. How many people did we lose? O'Brien?''

"Nearly half the roustabouts, Zach, but Sam's alive. He's hurt, but he's alive."

"Good. How about the men in the hold?"

"They're okay," Moore reported. "They got out when two of the hatch covers were destroyed."

"Good. Is the boat leaking?"

"Incredibly, no. The engine room's damaged, though. And the rest of the boat's a complete wreck."

O'Brien came up the stairs slowly. His head was bandaged with a rag and his shirt was badly torn. Blood had caked on his chest and arm.

"Sam," Cole greeted him with concern. "How bad is it?"

"I'll live."

"How about the engine room crew?"

"Three dead. Two badly wounded."

Cole nodded grimly. "And the engines?"

"Larboard engine is out of commission. The walking beam's gone and the connecting rod bent and splintered. But we may be able to salvage parts from the *Big Horn*."

"Okay. How about the sternwheel?"

"Same goes for that. We should be able to adapt parts of the *Big Horn's* wheel. It'll take time, but we should be able to do it."

"All right. And we'll have to repair the wheelhouse, too. Get started right away."

"Aye aye, sir."

His two subordinates left, passing Raasch as he came up the stairs. Raasch hardly glanced at Cole as he walked past him toward the salon doors. Cole followed.

Inside the salon Raasch stopped in front of Kingsley, who was rising from beside a fallen soldier, and saluted. "Sir," he said, "we have seven men fit for duty, including ourselves. All the others are dead or wounded."

"Very well. Is the fire on the *Big Horn* out?"

"Yes, sir. We could pull one of the guns out of the water, but there's no powder from the *Big Horn*; it all got blown into the river."

"All right. Leave it then. Any prisoners?"

"We found three Yankee soldiers unhurt. And most of the *Big Horn's* engine room crew survived. We also saved about six or seven wounded. And we found Major Van Hill."

"Alive?"

"Badly hurt, sir. Mostly burns."

"Put the major back in his old cabin," Kingsley said, "assuming there's still a bunk in it."

"Yes, sir. We'll start bringing the *Big Horn's* provisions over as soon as we're done getting the wounded settled."

"Very well. Carry on."

"Yes, sir." Raasch saluted, and Kingsley returned the gesture. Raasch turned to leave but stopped in front of Cole. "Sergeant Devlin said to tell you to watch your step comin' out of the wheelhouse," he growled.

Cole nodded. "I will." Somehow he was glad the sergeant was still alive.

"Good. Wouldn't want Devlin to kill you before I had the chance," Raasch said.

Cole sighed resignedly as Raasch walked away, then followed Kingsley down to the salon. "Colonel," Cole said.

Kingsley ignored him. Rebecca was kneeling beside a soldier who lay on a blanket on the carpeted deck. She was wrapping a strip of cloth torn from a sheet around the man's leg. He was the last in a long line of wounded men lying on the deck. Two Rebel soldiers were carrying a dead man from the far end of the line. Cole was appalled at how far the wounded stretched down the salon's deck.

"Hello, soldier," Kingsley addressed the man Rebecca was working on. "How are you?" he asked quietly.

"Okay, Colonel, I guess. We sure showed them Yankees, huh?"

"We sure did, son."

Rebecca finished tying the ends of the bandage. "There, that should do for now." She smiled weakly at the wounded man.

"Thank you, ma'am," the soldier said, forcing a grin.

Rebecca tried to stand, but faltered. Her father grabbed her arm and helped her to her feet.

"Are you all right, Rebecca?"

"I'll be all right, father," she said.

"How are the others?" Kingsley asked, nodding toward the double row of wounded.

"Father, those men need a doctor, not a nurse." All three of them watched a pair of Rebels bring a wounded Union soldier in on a stretcher and head for the end of the line.

"I know, I know," he said, putting an arm around her shoulders and patting her tenderly. "You've done a fine job. I'm proud of you."

Rebecca bowed her head in fatigue. "Thank you, father."

"I have duties elsewhere," he said.

She nodded, and Kingsley left. Cole didn't follow the colonel; his sympathy for Rebecca won out over his anger at Kingsley for the moment.

Rebecca went to another soldier lying quietly on the carpet beneath a blood-soaked blanket. Cole followed her.

"This boy is bleeding severely, Captain," she said, kneeling down. She put a hand on his forehead. "If he doesn't—"

She stopped and gasped, taking hold of his wrist. "Oh, no," she said.

Cole went around to the other side of the soldier and felt for a pulse, but there was none. "I'm afraid he's gone, Miss Kingsley," he said quietly.

Rebecca brushed the man's hair back from his forehead, then pulled the blanket over the still face. She stood up, sniffling. Looking down at him, she said, "I knew this boy.

I grew up with him. We played together as children.'' She sniffled again.

Cole stood up and came around to her. He wanted to put an arm around her, but he wasn't sure she would appreciate the gesture.

Tears rolled quietly down her cheeks. "Going off to save the Confederacy. Just like me, I guess. So young. And to die like this. He should have died in bed of old age, full of years and memories. At least my mother had done a lot more living than he had when she died.''

Cole felt like telling her that her father was responsible for the boy's death, that the boy's life had been wasted, that his death had been unnecessary and pointless. But telling her that now didn't seem appropriate. He just stood there.

Rebecca wiped her nose with the back of a bloody hand, and dabbed her eyes with a piece of cloth torn from the sheets. Holding the rag in one hand she walked slowly through the wrecked cabin and out onto the boiler deck promenade and stepped up to the railing.

Cole followed her again.

The early evening breeze fluffed out her hair and caressed her face. Wearily she stared out at the bluffs in the distance. "I wonder what those savages on the bluffs think of all this carnage?''

"They're probably flabbergasted,'' Cole said.

"Oh, Captain Cole,'' she murmured. "I'm so utterly sick of death. Of death, misery, pain, sadness. I'm sick, sick, sick of it.''

"There'll soon be an end to it,'' Cole said. "Even your father will have to see that the war is finished.''

"When mother was killed, I wanted the war to go on forever if necessary. I didn't care how many died, as long as the Confederacy survived. It was the only way that her sacrifice would have any meaning.''

She brought her hands up along her arms, holding them

tightly to herself while squeezing the rag into a little knot. She shuddered involuntarily.

Still looking at the shore, she continued. "But I'd never been so close to so much death before. My mother's death horrified me. But the rest of the deaths during the war meant little more to me than simply names in a newspaper. Now?" She slowly opened her arms and looked down at the blood smeared on her hands. "Now I recognize my mother's death as just one tiny drop of blood in an ocean of gore, an ocean that's still getting wider and deeper."

"Perhaps," ventured Cole, "you could persuade your father to stop now, before any more get killed for no reason."

After a moment she said, "He won't stop. He's become inured to death. It's a matter of honor with him."

Cole stepped closer still. He felt an almost uncontrollable urge to put his hands gently on her shoulders. "Is there anything I can do?"

"Yes," she said softly, turning around to look into his eyes with desperate pleading. "Get this boat to a doctor as fast as you can."

"We're still hundreds of miles away from Fort Benton," Cole told her.

"But what about the other forts along the river?" she asked.

Cole shook his head. "They can't do anything for us that we can't do for ourselves. They either don't have doctors, or the doctors they do have are drunken rejects, worse than none at all."

"But those men'll die without a doctor's attention," she insisted.

"Then they're going to die," Cole said softly.

She closed her eyes and leaned her head forward, resting it against Cole's chest.

Cole slowly brought his hands up and gently held her shoulders. "I'm sorry," he said.

"So am I," she said. "I am so sorry."

Chapter Fifteen

It took three days to repair the *West Wind's* engines and sternwheel as well as could be done. A large section of the starboard smokestack had to be cut off, which gave the steamboat an odd asymmetrical appearance. The other smokestack had been riddled as well, and with the diminished draft and the damage to the engines, the *West Wind* could only make half her previous speed. The *Big Horn*, therefore, was stripped of everything that wouldn't burn, making it easier to tow.

By the time the *West Wind* once again was headed upstream, three more of the wounded had died. And they continued to die in the following days. At night, while the *West Wind* was anchored in midstream, a detail would be sent out to bury another corpse ashore, with the hope that the angry Sioux would not be able to find and desecrate the grave the next morning.

The *West Wind* met the *Mountain Queen* coming down the river, her decks populated with miners who had wintered over in the goldfields of Montana, and her strongbox bulging with gold dust and nuggets.

A warning shot across the *Mountain Queen's* bows beached her immediately, but Captain Joshua Holt was belligerent when Raasch brought him back to the *West Wind*. And Raasch was sullen.

Holt wagged a newspaper in Kingsley's face. "Read it yourself, Colonel," he demanded, pronouncing the title with scorn. "The Confederacy is dead."

"It's a lie!" Kingsley shouted back.

"It is not!" Holt threw the newspaper at Kingsley's chest, and the officer clutched at it reflexively. "Read it, read it!"

Kingsley fumbled with the paper and opened the folded newsprint to the front page. "How did you get a St. Louis paper way up here?" he asked suspiciously.

"It comes overland through Wyoming Territory. Then up to Helena and then to Fort Benton," Holt explained smugly.

Kingsley's worried eyes scanned the newspaper. "May tenth," he mumbled. "President Davis captured by Federal cavalry."

"Two weeks ago," Cole said numbly. He thought of all the men who had died on the two steamboats in the battle, after Davis had already been captured.

"Yes," Holt confirmed, "and Johnston surrendered to Sherman long ago. Where have you been?"

Kingsley crumpled the newspaper with grim determination.

"Wait," Holt said. He snatched the paper from Kingsley's hands and smoothed it out. "There's even an article about you in here."

"Me?" a surprised Kingsley asked weakly.

Holt shuffled through the pages. "Here," he said, folding the newspaper back. "On page six." He handed the paper to Kingsley. "Read that." He jabbed a finger at a lower corner of the page.

Kingsley forced himself to read the article. Then he closed his eyes and took a deep breath. "Dishonor. They've lumped me together with the likes of those cutthroats Quantrill and Bloody Bill Anderson."

"There's no Confederate government anymore," Captain Holt declared. "No Confederate armies, no Confederacy. You've no authority, no sanction. You're an outlaw."

Kingsley stared at Holt, his brow knit. He glanced at his men, who returned the worried look.

Kingsley crushed the newspaper and let it drop to the deck. "The war is over," he said softly. "The war is really over."

Cole felt a twinge of compassion for the man whose whole reason for being had suddenly vanished. But it was only a passing emotion.

Kingsley sighed. "Well." He turned slowly and raised his head proudly to scan the men gathered in a rough semicircle before him.

Rebecca appeared at the boiler deck railing. Cole noticed that her face was contorted in anguish. He wondered if it was for her father or for the Confederacy. Probably for both, he decided.

"Soldiers of the Confederacy," Kingsley began. "We have fought long and hard for our righteous cause, but our sacrifice, and that of thousands of our brothers in arms, has proved insufficient. The Confederacy is dead. And our mission is no longer meaningful or lawful."

There was a disturbed murmur from his audience.

"Let me say that I feel deeply honored and fortunate to have served with such a gallant and devoted regiment and particularly with you men here, who chose to accompany me on this most hazardous mission."

"We'd follow you anywhere, Colonel."

"You led us good."

Kingsley held up a hand. "Thank you, men. Thank you for your loyalty."

"What do we do now, Colonel?"

"Honor and military convention dictate that we surrender to the nearest United States military authority."

"Surrender?" The word was repeated with distaste.

"But I am appalled at the idea of surrendering this gallant force to the scum of the Union Army out here," Kingsley added. "So I won't."

The men cheered.

"I will not resist arrest if confronted by a force sufficient to prevent our escape, but neither will I seek out incarceration.''

Another Rebel cheer.

"However, we must stop at once the confiscation and destruction of property of the citizens of the United States. Furthermore, I will turn over to Captain Holt all valuables confiscated by us so far. He will be charged with delivering them to the proper United States authorities so that they may be returned to their previous owners.''

"Give it back?'' someone mumbled. "After all we went through to get it?''

"Think of all of us who've died, Colonel.''

Cole didn't think much of giving it to Holt for safekeeping either. He doubted that any of it would get back to previous owners, even if Holt could figure out who the owners were.

Kingsley went on, ignoring the protests of his men. "We will transfer all of our wounded, blue and gray, to the *Mountain Queen*. She can make it to medical aid faster than we can. This boat can barely move.''

"What happens to us?''

"Every man must decide for himself what he is to do. I, personally, can never live under United States authority again. I intend to travel to Canada.''

"Canada?''

Kingsley turned toward Cole. "Captain Cole, how far are we from Fort Benton?''

"About 650 miles,'' Cole told him.

"Still? Seems like we've come half way round the world by now. And every mile hungry for wood. Well, no matter. At what point does the Missouri come closest to the Canadian border?''

"You have to go almost all the way to Fort Benton,'' Cole said. "You'd be about sixty or seventy miles from the border.''

"Hah,'' Kingsley said. "We can march that in two days.''

"Colonel," Devlin spoke up. "I'm sorry, sir, but I don't want to go to Canada. I've got a wife and two kids back home."

"That will be up to you," Kingsley said. "No man need go to Canada who doesn't want to. I understand your desire to return to your families and homes. But I have neither to return to. My home is destroyed, and I have my family with me."

"Why can't we just turn around and go back home, Colonel?" a corporal asked. It was Murphy.

"We've been branded—unjustifiably—as outlaws, not soldiers," Kingsley said. "To simply turn the boat around and go back downstream will land us all in prison—or worse."

There was a general mumbling among the soldiers.

"No Yankee prison for me."

Kingsley held up his hand again for silence. "And you cannot simply abandon the river and head back overland." He pointed to the hills. "The Sioux. We are now so few that we would not be a match for them. Therefore we must stay with the boat."

"What do you suggest, Colonel?"

"Go with me to Fort Benton and scatter among the mining camps. From there make your way home as best you can individually. The United States authorities will never be able to figure out that you were the ones on this mission, so you will be able to live in security from then on."

Heads nodded.

"Colonel," Raasch said. "About this givin' the gold back."

"We shall return the gold and the money, Captain Raasch," Kingsley said. "Honor requires that."

"But wait a minute," Raasch said. He stepped forward. "You said yourself the Confederacy is dead. And so's the Confederate Army. So we're no longer in an army, and you don't have the final word on everything anymore."

"Captain!" Kingsley bristled.

Raasch turned to the others. "I don't know about you boys, but I have no intention of givin' back what we've got up in that strongbox, and I think we oughta relieve the *Mountain Queen* of her gold, too."

"What?" Holt blurted. His folded arms uncrossed and his hands dropped to his sides.

"Taking that gold now would make us common criminals indeed," asserted Kingsley.

"Well, so what?" Raasch snapped. "The Yankees consider us outlaws already."

"Those valuables were not taken for our personal enrichment, Captain," Kingsley said angrily. "They were seized to help the Confederacy. There is no Confederacy any longer, so—"

"Wait a minute, Colonel," Devlin put in. "The Confederacy maybe doesn't need that gold anymore, but the South sure does."

Kingsley turned on the sergeant. "I did not ask for your opinion, Sergeant Devlin."

"Them Yankees ruined my farm," Devlin went on. "They run off my stock, trampled the crops, burned my barn. Why, my family's been livin' off the charity of neighbors for a long time. I was willin' to let 'em live in shame like that just so's I could keep fightin'. But the fightin's over now, and it's been for nothin' anyway it seems. And even a small share of that gold would go a long way toward fixin' up my farm."

"Dishonor!" Kingsley's face was getting red. "A man cannot live without honor."

"Well, maybe I don't feel as honorable as you do, Colonel," Devlin said. "It's Yankees that ruined my farm, and I think it's Yankees that oughta buy me a new one. I'm not for takin' any more, but I'm not for givin' back any we got already. We didn't know the war was over. Besides, how are we gonna get it back to those we took it from?"

Cole had to grin in appreciation. Devlin was no fool.

"I wouldn't mind goin' back home with a pocketful of gold," Murphy commented.

"Me? I'd head for San Francisco," another soldier added.

"I'm in command here," Kingsley roared, "and I say the gold goes back!"

"Nobody's givin' orders to me anymore," Raasch declared.

"How dare you?" Rebecca screamed from the boiler deck railing. Everyone looked up, surprised by the outburst. "How dare you challenge my father like that. All of you. But particularly you, Captain Raasch. You who owe so much to him. You ought to get down on your knees and beg—"

"Don't get high and mighty with me, little Miss Stuckup," Raasch hurled back. "Those days are gone forever."

Kingsley drew his pistol and swung it, catching Raasch on the side of the head. The captain hit the deck and rolled onto his side, grimacing and holding his head.

"Don't you speak to my daughter like that!" Kingsley roared, his face red with anger.

"Hold it, hold it, Colonel," Devlin said, stepping forward. "The captain's right. The war's over, and we're all really private citizens again."

Kingsley whirled and took a step toward his sergeant. "Insubordination!" the colonel shouted.

A shot rang out, and everybody flinched as a bullet tore into Kingsley's back and ripped a bloody hole in the front of his tunic. Kingsley grunted and pitched forward to collapse in Devlin's arms.

"Father!" Rebecca screamed. She raced for the stairs.

Angrily, Devlin looked down at Raasch and the smoking pistol in his hand. "Why'd you do that?" he demanded. "I was in no danger." He lowered Kingsley gently to the deck.

Others of Kingsley's men grumbled, and some started bringing their rifles up.

Raasch jumped to his feet and pointed his pistol at Devlin. "Nobody takes a hand to me, not even Kingsley." Devlin halted.

Cole quickly knelt down over Kingsley to examine the wound. Rebecca sank to the deck and grasped her father's head in her hands.

"Oh, father, father. Not you, too."

"He's not dead, Miss Kingsley," Cole told her. "The bullet went clear through him. Came out his shoulder. The angle means the bullet probably missed his vital parts. But he's going to bleed badly."

"Now listen to me," Raasch shouted to the Rebels. "We're gonna keep everything in the strongbox in Cole's office, and we're gonna take everything in the *Mountain Queen's* safe. When we get to Fort Benton we'll divide it all up amongst ourselves."

"Wait a minute, Raasch," Devlin said. "Why should we follow your say any more than we should take orders from the Colonel now? At least him I respected."

"Because I'm doin' what you want to do."

"What kind of split you thinkin' about, Captain?" Murphy asked tentatively.

"An equal split. There's plenty for all of us, and we all suffered together."

Someone whistled. "That'd be a good stake."

"Well, are you with me?" Raasch asked.

"You shouldn't've shot the colonel, Captain," one man said.

"Do you think you could ever have talked him into letting you keep the gold for your families?" Raasch argued. "Besides, he's not dead, just wounded. I could just as easily have put that bullet through his heart."

"Well, boys," Murphy said, "I think we deserve that gold. What do you think, Sergeant Devlin?"

Cole looked at the sergeant. He could see that Devlin was struggling. Loyal to his colonel, he had a family to consider, too. And what good would giving the gold back do?

"Maybe the captain's right," Devlin said softly.

"That's good enough for me," Murphy declared. "I'm in with you, Captain Raasch."

"We're all with you, Captain," another soldier said, though he sounded reluctant.

"San Francisco, here I come," said another, this one with conviction.

Rebecca cradled her father's head. "How quickly they forget him," she said to Cole. Tears were rolling down her cheeks.

Cole was stuffing a handkerchief inside the colonel's tunic, though he doubted that would do much good. "They're scared and confused," he said.

"All right," said Raasch. "Let's get moving." He stepped in front of Holt. "Captain, I'm takin' your steamboat. We can't depend on getting wood, so we need the steamboat for fuel, and this boat's in too bad condition to tow a boat anymore. We need a boat that can steam on her own power along with the *WestWind*. You can have the *Big Horn*."

Holt, wide-eyed, looked back at the hulk attached to the towing line from the *West Wind*. The *Big Horn* had been cut down to the main deck by now, all her superstructure having been fed into the *West Wind's* fireboxes.

"But that thing can't do more than just float," Holt protested. "No engines, no—"

"You don't have to go anywhere, Captain," Raasch told him. "Just sit there anchored in the middle of the river."

"What about the Indians, Raasch?" Cole asked, standing up. He walked over to the two men. "You just can't leave all those people to the mercy of the Sioux."

"I won't," argued Raasch. "They can stay in the hold

to keep from getting shot. And I'll leave 'em their arms and some ammunition. Besides, the Indians don't want them; they want us, remember. And I'll give 'em plenty of provisions. We'll take the wounded with us.''

"But what are we to do?" Holt asked, holding his hands out helplessly.

"You wait. Once we get to Fort Benton, the *Mountain Queen*—or what's left of her—will come back downstream for you.''

Holt blustered. "But that could be a month.''

"Another boat might come upstream," Raasch said. He looked at Cole. "Mostly it depends on him. The faster he gets us to Fort Benton, the faster he can come back for you.''

Cole knew that Raasch would try to kill him once they reached Fort Benton. But at least someone could come back down. He looked at Holt. "Three weeks.''

Holt's shoulders sagged. "Or maybe six.''

"All right, let's move," Raasch shouted. "Enough out of you, Holt. Another word and you'll be floating face down in the river.''

Holt drew back and fell silent.

Raasch put everyone to work. All the passengers and most of the crew of the *Mountain Queen* were transferred to the hulk of the *Big Horn*, along with a supply of food. The crew and passengers would be given their weapons when the *West Wind* left.

Much of the provisions from the *Mountain Queen* were transferred to the *West Wind*, as well as all of her wood. Raasch instructed the roustabouts to start tearing the *Mountain Queen* apart for fuel. And all the gold in the *Mountain Queen's* safe was stuffed into the strongbox in Cole's office cabin.

Cole checked in on Van Hill on the *West Wind*. "How are you doing, Major?" he asked from the side of his bunk. Van Hill was obviously in a lot of pain. Rebecca had put only light bandages on him because he couldn't stand to have anything touch his burned skin.

"I hurt pretty bad," the officer said weakly. "How much longer before we get to Fort Benton?"

"Couple of weeks, I'm afraid." He straightened out the blanket at the foot of the bed. "Ironic thing is, Major, that Jefferson Davis had already been captured."

"Yes, I know," Van Hill said.

"You know?" Cole asked with a frown.

"Yes, they told us at Fort Sully."

"But—But—" Cole sputtered, "that meant the war was over. Even Kingsley admits that. He would have surrendered to any show of force. Why didn't you try talking instead of charging with cannons blazing?"

"Who would've remembered the officer who merely accepted Kingsley's surrender?" Van Hill asked. "No, I had to capture him in a fight. It was my last chance to get my good name back."

"But dozens of men died in that fight, Major," Cole exclaimed. "Dozens."

Van Hill closed his eyes. "I had to take the risk."

Cole was speechless. He stared down at the man, at his bandaged wounds, the burned flesh on his face. And he thought of the carnage the battle had produced. He turned and stalked out.

He headed for Kingsley's cabin. There he found both Devlin and Rebecca standing at the side of Kingsley's bunk. The colonel was awake, lying on his side facing the bulkhead with his bare back to the occupants of the compartment. Rebecca was washing Kingsley's back gently.

"How is he?" Cole asked Devlin.

Before Devlin could answer, Kingsley spoke. "I am alive, Captain," he said.

Rebecca pressed a fresh cloth to the wound, which was still bleeding profusely.

Devlin sighed. "Colonel, that wound's going to bleed a

lot. You're gonna have to lie real still to give it a chance to close.''

Kingsley nodded. ''I've seen as many wounds as you have, Sergeant.''

''Yes, sir.''

''Help me roll on my back.''

Devlin's strong hands eased the colonel onto his back. Kingsley let out a groan of pain.

Devlin asked, ''Anything else I can do for you, Colonel?'' Kingsley shook his head. Devlin looked at Rebecca. ''Call me if you need any more help, Miss Rebecca.''

Rebecca nodded. ''Thank you, Sergeant.''

Devlin touched the bill of his cap and exited the cabin.

Cole looked down at Kingsley. ''Is there anything I can do, Miss Kingsley?''

''Yes,'' Rebecca answered. ''Get us to Fort Benton and a doctor as fast as possible. For my father and Major Van Hill and the four wounded men in the salon who might make it if a doctor could operate on them.''

''I'll do my best,'' Cole said. He left the cabin.

On the main deck he found Devlin again. The sergeant was supervising the placing of the four wounded men on the deck planking just abaft of the forward storage compartment.

''Why have you moved them down here from the salon where they had shelter?'' Cole asked.

Devlin finished adjusting the blankets under one unconscious man. ''Captain,'' he said, rising, ''whenever one of our boys went to a hospital, he never came back. And up there reminds 'em too much of a hospital. So they'll take their chances in the open air down here.''

''I see.''

''Cole!'' It was Raasch.

''What do you want?'' Cole asked. He noticed that Raasch was now carrying Cole's Henry rifle.

''We're ready to go.''

"All right. I'm going to make a quick trip over to the *Mountain Queen* to talk to her pilot," Cole said. "He can tell me what to expect upstream."

"He's not there," Raasch told him. "He's on the *Big Horn*."

"The *Big Horn*?" Cole asked in surprise. "What's he doing there? Who's going to pilot the *Mountain Queen*?"

"Moore."

Cole gaped. "He's no pilot."

"That's why I put him there. He knows he'd never make it down the river by himself, so he won't get any idea of organizin' an attack on the three men I've got over there and runnin' away with the boat."

"Moore's bound to hit something, Raasch."

"Not if he just tags along right behind you. If he goes where you go, he'll be all right."

"It's not that simple," Cole argued.

"Raasch," Devlin said, "I still say it would be better to keep the *Mountain Queen's* pilot or maybe that Kellogg fellow. Harris and the others can watch a pilot as well as the engineer."

"No," Raasch said. "They all go on the *Big Horn*."

"You're putting Kellogg on the *Big Horn*, too?" Cole asked hopefully.

"Yeah, and Carpenter. They're just two extra mouths to feed."

"Then there's no one in the hold anymore," Cole said.

"No," Raasch said, "but I figure you don't need that anymore. There's no longer any reason for you to sink this boat. Just get us and the wounded to Fort Benton and you can have your boat back. That oughta be incentive enough for you to be careful."

"Yes, I suppose," Cole said. But he didn't know what good the boat would do him if Raasch shot him dead when they reached the fort.

Chapter Sixteen

Several nights later, with the *West Wind* quietly riding at anchor in midstream, Raasch, Devlin, and Murphy sat a small table in her salon. The Henry rifle lay on the table in front of Raasch. He drained the last of the whiskey from a bottle before him and disgustedly tossed the empty bottle against the shattered bar in the *West Wind's* salon. He turned to look at Devlin and Murphy.

"Wish more bottles had survived that fight with the *Big Horn*," he said.

Murphy poured more whiskey into a glass in front of him. "There ain't much else to do every night 'cept drink."

Devlin made no comment. He was staring blankly out through the jagged holes in a bulkhead made by the *Big Horn's* shot.

Raasch grabbed the bottle from Murphy.

"Hey," Murphy complained. But he didn't follow up on his protest.

"After we get to Fort Benton," Raasch said, "I'm never gonna set foot on another steamboat." He took a swig from the bottle and slammed it down on the tabletop. He stared over at the door of Kingsley's cabin.

"We oughta ask Miss Stuck-up to come out here and entertain us."

"You're drunk, Raasch," Devlin charged. He still stared at the bulkhead.

"What if I am?" Raasch asked angrily, looking at the sergeant.

"If you were sober you wouldn't even think of somethin' like that. She's quality and you're white trash just like the rest of us."

"I'm an officer and a gentleman," Raasch declared. He leaned across the table and shook a fist in Devlin's face. "Devlin, I'm gonna—"

"Hey," Murphy interrupted. "I got enough of a headache without you two chawin' at each other all the time."

Raasch slouched backwards. He shrugged. "It's time for you to leave anyway," he said.

Devlin and Murphy both looked out through assorted holes in the bulkheads. "Looks about as dark as it's gonna get," Murphy said. "Wish there wasn't any moon at all."

"Raasch," Devlin asked, "why don't you take one of the burial details?"

"Because I told *you* to, that's why."

"You're not an officer anymore."

Murphy grabbed Devlin's arm. "Aw, come on, Sergeant," he urged. "Let's put poor Loomis to his rest."

Devlin sighed. "Just two more wounded left down there." He rose. "Okay, Murphy, let's go."

Devlin and Murphy rose and left the salon. Raasch threw the now empty bottle into a corner of the salon and slumped forward on his elbows on the table. His blurred gaze fell on Kingsley's door again. He sat there for a moment, thinking of the cabin's occupants.

He rose, scraping the chair away roughly, sauntered unsteadily to Kingsley's cabin, and rapped on the door. "Miss Kingsley." There was no answer so he opened the door. Rebecca was sitting in a chair.

"What do you want, Captain Raasch?" she asked coldly, looking up at him.

In the dark cabin, Raasch couldn't see her face, but the disapproving tone of her voice was unmistakable. It incensed him.

He stepped inside. "Good evenin'," he said with extreme politeness.

"You've got a lot of nerve coming in here, Captain."

"Now, nobody need get hurt, if you'll just cooperate." He started toward her.

Rebecca's chair creaked as she stiffened. "You would violate me in the same room where my father lies dying from a bullet you put through him?"

Raasch glanced at the unconscious form on the bunk. The bandage on Kingsley shoulder was soaked with blood, as was the sheet beneath him. "He won't be offended,"

"I'd die rather than submit to you," Rebecca declared. She gripped the arms of the chair.

Raasch reached down for her arm and yanked her violently to her feet. She let out a short, sharp gasp of pain. "I mean to take you down a peg or two," he growled. "Teach you some respect for me."

Rebecca spat in his eyes. Her hands flew to his face, and her nails dug into his flesh.

He yelled and jerked his head away, then slapped her across the face.

Rebecca staggered backward and bumped into the washstand, rattling a bowl and pitcher that sat on it. She groped in the dark for the pitcher, seized it, swung it in a wide arc, and broke it against Raasch's head as he came at her.

Raasch staggered backwards, holding his head with both hands, whimpering angrily.

Rebecca rushed for the outside cabin door. She managed to open it, but Raasch grabbed her savagely by the hair and yanked her back. She cried in pain, and tears came to her eyes. Her hands clawed the air to get at his wrists, but he threw her against the bulkhead. She winced at the impact, and the air was knocked from her lungs.

Raasch slammed his massive body into her, crushing her against the bulkhead, burying his face in her hair. Rebecca struggled desperately. She tossed her head violently from side to side, pulled at Raasch's hair, clawed at his face, hissed, and snarled at him. But his strength was overwhelming.

Two strong hands clamped down on Raasch's shoulders and jerked him away from Rebecca.

Raasch growled and turned, an arm cocked back for a punch, but Cole's fist smashed into his face. Raasch staggered backward and collided with the doorjamb of the inside cabin doorway. He crashed to the deck with a moan.

The startled man felt his jaw in agony. "Cole! That's twice you hit me." He pulled out his pistol and cocked it. "So I'm gonna put two bullets in you." He raised the pistol.

Cole kicked violently. The pistol fired as it left Raasch's hand to somersault through the open door and land on the carpet in the salon. The bullet lodged in the doorjamb.

Raasch clutched his injured wrist and cursed. He was halfway to his feet when Cole's boot drove into his chest. The man hurtled out of the cabin and fell over backward.

Cole rushed out of the cabin, but Raasch was now alert. He leaped to his feet and met Cole's charge head on. The two men toppled to the deck and rolled as they pummeled each other, crunching over debris, bumping into the table holding Cole's Henry rifle. Finally they knocked the table over, and the rifle clattered to the floor.

Raasch heaved Cole off of him. The Confederate rolled and came up with the rifle. Cole grabbed a broken board as he jumped to his feet.

But Raasch was up, too. And he brought the cocked rifle to bear on Cole just as the latter had the board poised over his head to bring it down on Raasch's. Cole froze.

Raasch laughed. "Cole, I'm gonna kill you with your own rifle."

A pistol fired, and a bullet whizzed past Raasch's face.

Both Raasch and Cole jerked their heads around. They saw Van Hill standing near the doorway of Kingsley's cabin.

With his white, partly naked body, bandages, and a sheet, he looked like a specter from the dead.

But he was pointing Raasch's pistol at the Confederate's head, holding the gun with both hands. Desperately he tried to cock the pistol with his weakened hands, grimacing from the effort.

Raasch turned the Henry and fired. The bullet slammed Van Hill against the bulkhead. His hands sailed over his head and the pistol fired straight up into the air. Van Hill crumpled to the deck.

Raasch levered another cartridge into the Henry's chamber and spun the Henry around, but he wasn't quick enough. Cole broke the board over Raasch's head and drove him to the deck. He lay still, but he was still breathing.

Cole straightened up and caught his breath. He tossed the board away and picked up the Henry, giving the barrel a quick caress. It felt good to have its power in his hands again.

Cole hurried over to Van Hill and knelt down. It was dark in the salon, but Cole could make out the fresh bullet wound in the man's chest. He was dead.

"Thanks, Major," he said softly.

He got to his feet and entered Kingsley's cabin. Rebecca was bending over her father's figure on the bunk. She was dabbing at the blood that still seeped from his shoulder wound.

"He's lost so much blood already."

Cole was not optimistic about Kingsley's fate, but he said nothing about it. "Miss Kingsley," he said. "I've got my boat back, and I mean to keep it." He hefted the Henry. "If Devlin and the others won't surrender when they get back, I plan to fight them. This rifle is a match for all them."

Rebecca looked at Cole in some confusion.

"And I'm going to tie up Raasch out there, before he wakes up and tries to kill me again."

She nodded weakly, but she was puzzled.

"What about you?" he asked. "Do I have to worry about you behind my back?"

"Oh." Rebecca didn't hesitate with her answer. "I only care about getting my father to a doctor. I don't care whose boat it is."

"Good."

Cole left the cabin, picked up Raasch's pistol and stuck it in his belt. He laid down the Henry and grabbed the unconscious Raasch under the armpits and dragged him toward an open cabin. He got him inside and stripped a sheet from the bunk in the cabin and started to tear the sheet into strips.

Cole froze when he heard a rifle being cocked. He looked up into the muzzle of Devlin's rifle.

"Captain Cole," Devlin said. "I don't much care for Raasch there, but him and me been through a lot of war together, and there ain't nothin' I hate worse than a Yankee."

Chapter Seventeen

Cole finished a futile inspection of the hatches; each cover had been weighted down to prevent his escape from the *West Wind's* hold. He sank down against a center post and stretched his legs out. There was little to see in the eerie glow of moonlight that filtered through cracks and shot holes in the deck above. Cole saw no hope in his situation either.

He supposed that he should have been grateful for even being alive. If it had not been for Van Hill, Raasch would have shot him back there.

Poor Nathan Van Hill. The man had been so desperate to get his name back, and now there would not even be a name on a headstone for a grave. Raasch had thrown his body overboard. True oblivion.

And Cole had Devlin and Murphy, who insisted that Cole was needed, to thank for Raasch not shooting him as soon as Raasch had recovered consciousness.

Now the reckless Raasch was piloting the steamboat himself—charging off into the night with the *Mountain Queen* trying frantically to catch up—just to show Devlin and Murphy that they didn't need Cole, so the two men wouldn't object to his shooting him. That had been half an hour ago. Cole knew it was only a matter of time before Raasch wrecked the boat.

With a splintering crash the jagged ends of the trunk of a sunken tree smashed through the thin planks of the *West Wind's* bow, cracking and ripping boards and bringing the steamboat to a sudden halt. The snag went right on up to pop off the cover of one of the forward hatches, tossing aside the box of shot as if it were empty.

Cole gasped at the sudden jolt and went sprawling. The river poured into the hold and a wall of water knocked him back in the other direction. But with a leap of hope Cole saw the open hatch.

He scrambled forward on his hands and knees, forcing his way through the deluge of water by pulling on the ribs of the boat. By the time he reached the open forward hatch, the water was already a foot deep in the hold.

He struggled through the limbs of the tree, fighting the rushing torrent that clawed at his legs and tried to pull him under, coughing and gulping in water.

Finally he squeezed himself through the space between the tree trunk and the hatch coaming. He saw some men scrambling up the forward stairs and heard Devlin shouting to get the wounded up from the main deck.

Cole pulled himself all the way up through the hatch and rolled onto the forecastle deck just as water started coming over the bow as the steamboat settled rapidly. Springing to his feet, he scurried under the boiler deck overhang. Air whistled out through the holes in the deck as water flooded the hold.

He had just gone past the boilers when the rising water reached the fireboxes. There was a tremendous hissing roar as the cold river water swamped the red hot coals and hot iron. The water boiled and frothed and sputtered, and the iron plates buckled and pinged. Cole ran through ankle deep water, expecting the boilers to split open any second. But they held, booming and hissing and cracking as they contracted rapidly.

The engines stopped as the steam pressure dropped to zero. The sternwheel stopped turning and Cole flattened himself against the engine room bulkhead.

The boat sank deeper, throwing up vast bubbles of air,

churning the surface of the water and setting adrift boards, rope, and wooden debris. The cannon at the bow sank out of sight.

Cole jumped to the bull rails and grabbed a stationary to keep from being swept away. He expected the boat to stop sinking at any moment. There were few places in the entire Missouri deep enough to actually cover a whole steamboat, and there weren't too many places this far north that could do much more than cover the main deck.

But the *West Wind* kept sinking. Cole floated in the cold water, hanging onto the stationary, ready to grab the boiler deck railing as the water rose. When the forward section of the boiler deck had submerged, and there was only a foot of clearance between the boiler deck's after section and the water, the steamboat finally stopped settling.

A gurgling, violent foaming of water continued as more air escaped from the hold and from nooks and crannies of the main deck compartments, belching up more debris. Gradually the noise subsided, and soon all Cole could hear was the quiet lapping of the Missouri's water against the superstructure bulkheads and the angry voices of an argument between Raasch and Devlin on the hurricane deck.

"How could you be so stupid?" Devlin screamed. "Cole never ran at night. What made you think you could?"

"Shut up, Devlin," Raasch shouted back. A pistol fired. "As long as I'm giving the orders—"

"You talk mighty big with a gun in your hand, Raasch."

"That's right," Raasch agreed. "Now get going. We gotta get ready to hop onto the *Mountain Queen* when she comes alongside."

Cole stayed in the water. There was enough room between the overhang of the boiler deck and the water's surface to let him stay out of sight and still breathe easily. He just wished the water weren't so cold.

"Where's that engineer, O'Brien?" Raasch asked when he and Devlin reached the boiler deck.

"Dead," Devlin reported. "That rooster, Josh, says that when we hit, the engineer was knocked right into one of the engines and got his neck broken."

"Mm. Too bad."

"And Turner and Poole both got washed overboard. I couldn't get down there in time."

"Now that I am sorry about. They were good men."

"And they'd still be alive if you'd listened to me."

"Oh, shut up. Did we lose any of those roustabouts?"

"No, but Cole's dead, Raasch. Down in the hold, remember?" Raasch's voice was more cheerful. "That's right!"

"Cole was a pilot, Raasch, and you just proved you're not."

"Shut up, Devlin. How many times I gotta tell you that. Murphy, go get the strongbox from Cole's office and drag it out to the boiler deck railing. We'll board the *Mountain Queen* when she comes alongside."

"Yes, sir." The three men headed for the boiler deck.

Rebecca mounted the hurricane deck. "Captain Raasch."

"What do you want, Miss Stuck-up?" Raasch asked.

"You must help me get my father out of here."

Raasch snorted. "We're not takin' dead men with us."

"He's not dead."

"He will be soon."

Devlin spoke up. "I'll help you, Miss Rebecca. Raasch, you can't just leave the man here."

"Yes, I can. I can leave anybody here I want, including," he emphasized, "little Miss Stuck-up there."

"Now you're really talkin' nonsense, Raasch," Devlin said.

Murphy called from the boiler deck. "We got the strongbox, Captain."

"Okay. I'll be right down. Here comes the *Mountain Queen.*"

Cole looked back and suddenly felt very vulnerable.

"Hey, back off," Raasch bellowed at the onrushing steamboat. He was rushing down the stairs. Devlin and Rebecca raced after him.

Moore was no pilot; he drove the *Mountain Queen* right into the *West Wind*, caving in the boiler deck railing and buckling the planking.

"Back off!" Raasch roared.

The *Mountain Queen* lost headway from the collision and started slowly crunching her way aft along the *West Wind's* side.

"Come on, everybody," Raasch said. "Throw that box onto the other boat and get aboard."

Cole heard the box crash down onto the deck of the *Mountain Queen.*

"Jump aboard!" Raasch barked. Roustabouts and Rebel soldiers leaped from one boat to the other.

"Raasch!" It was Moore in the wheelhouse on the *Mountain Queen.* "Where's Captain Cole?"

"He's okay."

"Where is he? I'm not goin' anywhere till I know."

"He's already aboard," Raasch said. "He'll be up there right away. Now get back to that wheel and head upriver."

Moore was quiet.

"Captain Raasch," Rebecca declared shrilly, "you will take my father aboard that boat this instant."

"Goodbye, Miss Stuck-up." Raasch leaped to the *Mountain Queen.*

"Come on, Miss Rebecca," Devlin said. "I'll help you with your father. But we gotta hurry."

"Devlin," Raasch shouted. "I'm not takin' him aboard."

"We'll see about that." Devlin's voice was muffled as he and Rebecca entered Kingsley's cabin.

The *Mountain Queen* started edging forward again. "Come on, Devlin," Raasch shouted. "Leave him."

Devlin and Rebecca appeared in the doorway of Kingsley's cabin with the colonel propped up against Devlin's shoulder. Rebecca helped as best she could.

"Raasch, stop that boat!" yelled Devlin. "Gimme a hand."

"Better get aboard, Devlin," Raasch shouted. "I'm not waiting."

"Raasch!" Devlin shouted once more.

The *Mountain Queen's* stern was brushing past the forward end of the *West Wind's* superstructure.

"Miss Rebecca," Devlin said in anguish. "I got a family back home. The *Mountain Queen* isn't much of a chance, but it's all there is."

"I understand, Sergeant," Rebecca said. "Thank you at least for trying."

"I'm sorry."

"Bless you, Sergeant, but go. Go!"

Devlin released Kingsley and Rebecca was unable to hold his weight. Kingsley slumped to the deck in six inches of water.

Devlin ran down the submerged boiler deck, leaping to the railing of the *West Wind*, and sprang for the outrigger of the *Mountain Queen*. His hands barely caught it, and he fell into the water, but he still hung on. He managed to pull himself up onto the boat despite the churning of the water by the sternwheel a foot away. "I'm sorry, Miss Rebecca," he shouted through cupped hands.

Rebecca waved forlornly to the sergeant. She watched the *Mountain Queen* churn her way into the night, her frothy wake glistening in the dim moonlight. When Rebecca could no longer make out Devlin's figure on the outrigger, she turned to the task of getting her father back into his bunk.

She struggled to pull him up, but his weight was too great for her. He slid to the deck and she plopped down in the water. "Oh, father," she murmured. She put an arm around his shoulder and rested his head on her shoulder.

Dripping cold water, a shivering Cole climbed onto the

boiler deck. He walked forward, stripping water from his clothes with his hands.

"Captain Cole," Rebecca exclaimed. She struggled to her feet, making sure her father didn't fall. "You're supposed to be dead. How'd you get out of the hold?"

"I climbed a tree," he explained, stopping before her.

"What?"

"Never mind," he said with a grin. He squatted down next to Kingsley. "How is he?"

"The same," she said. "Slipping. Pulse weak, still losing blood from the slightest movement."

"Miss Kingsley, you really should've gone with the *Mountain Queen*," Cole said.

"And leave him here? Never."

Cole smiled. "Your father's daughter," he said. But then he turned grim. "Miss Kingsley, I doubt your father will last much longer. If you'd gone on the *Mountain Queen*, at least you would have been alive."

"Hmph. And how long is the *Mountain Queen* going to last anyway? Raasch sank this boat and he'll probably sink that one, too, if he keeps running at night."

Cole nodded. "Good point."

Rebecca suddenly looked at Cole in shock. "But why did you stay here? They would have been delighted to have you on the other boat. I think Devlin and the others would have shot Raasch if they had had to."

Cole shrugged. "I don't know. I guess it just didn't occur to me to leave you and . . . "

Rebecca stared at him, and he stared back, his mind reeling with a sudden revelation.

He stood up. "Let's get your father out of the water."

With Rebecca's assistance, Cole soon had the wounded man lying on his bunk once more. Rebecca covered him with a blanket, then sloshed her way slowly back out to the boiler deck promenade. She stared at the dim bluffs in the distance.

"Do you suppose the Indians have gone by now?" she asked.

"No, not all of them," Cole answered. "Indians are great scavengers. In a couple of days they'll have this boat picked clean."

"Do they know we're aboard?"

"Maybe, maybe not. But they'll come aboard whether they think anyone is here or not."

"I see." She was silent for a moment. "How long before they'll try?"

"I'd say they'll wait until morning. That'll give 'em enough time to figure out how many of us there are. After they see how few we are . . . "

"Then our lives may be measured in hours, Captain. Any chance of another steamboat coming up before that?"

"No," Cole said softly. "But there is one chance, Miss Kingsley."

She turned to look at him hopefully. "There is?"

"We still have the boat's yawls. If we were to get into one of them this instant, we might be able to slip away from here in the dark without the Sioux noticing. If we make it to the *Big Horn* we'll be safe."

"How long would that take?"

"Couple of days, maybe."

"You really think we could make it?"

Cole took a deep breath. "If we're not seen. Otherwise the Sioux might swim out to intercept us. We have no weapons."

"I see." She didn't seem enthusiastic. "It doesn't sound hopeful. Well, I won't leave here without father anyway."

"We could take him along with us."

"No, it would kill him quickly. Just taking him to the door and back has started the blood flowing again."

"You're being very stubborn," Cole said in exasperation.

Thaddius Kingsley stirred and spoke. "Rebecca," he rasped.

His daughter rushed back into the cabin to his side, and Cole followed her. "Father, you're awake." She took hold of one of his hands.

"Daughter," Kingsley said, "I heard what Captain Cole said."

"Father, I won't leave you."

Kingsley coughed and grimaced. "You're kind, daughter, but I have seen too many deaths on the battlefield not to recognize my own imminent demise."

Rebecca turned to Cole with anguish in her eyes. Cole shifted his gaze to his feet, still under the cold Missouri River water.

"Rebecca," Kingsley ordered. "Do as Captain Cole says. Take the yawl while it is still dark."

"No," the woman answered. "It would kill you."

"Leave me."

"No!"

"Don't be foolish, daughter. I've had my life. And now it's over. Save yours."

"No, I have nothing to live for."

"Yes, you do. You are young. You can start over. The end of the war and of the Confederacy and of me need not be your end, also."

"No," she said firmly, shaking her head slowly.

Kingsley paused. He closed his eyes and took a deep breath. He let it out slowly in little painful bursts. "Rebecca, go to your cabin. I wish to speak to Captain Cole alone."

Rebecca looked puzzled. She glanced at Cole, but he only shrugged. "All right," she said. She let go of her father's hand and slowly sloshed her way out of the cabin.

Cole came closer. "Yes, Colonel?"

"Why did you stay on the boat when everyone else had left?"

"It's my boat, I guess."

"No." Kingsley broke into a spasm of coughing. "I'll tell you why you stayed. It was because of my daughter."

Cole was silent for a moment. "All right," he admitted. "It wasn't the boat. It was Rebecca."

Kingsley was breathing heavily and with effort. "A measure of a man's freedom is the way he chooses to die, Captain. I do not choose to die at the hands of the Sioux. Or by the hand of the likes of Captain Raasch. Nor do I choose to die in such a way as to endanger my daughter. She will not leave this boat with you unless I am dead. Therefore I must die now. Captain, you must kill me."

Cole was stunned. "Colonel?"

"Sir, you can see that I am helpless. I have not the strength to even fall out of bed and drown myself at your feet."

"But I can't just—"

"There's a knife in the drawer of that table, Captain," Kingsley told him. "I carried it with me all through the war. Get it."

Cole went to the drawer and opened it. He pulled out the leather sheath and withdrew a long-bladed knife.

"We will all benefit, Captain. I will be released from pain, and you and my daughter will have a chance to escape in the yawl. I only ask that it be painless." He rolled his head to the side to expose the artery in his neck.

Cole looked down. The man's heart must have been working hard at the moment, for the artery in his neck throbbed vigorously. Cole tried to visualize slicing through that life while its owner lay contently letting him do it. "Colonel, I can't do this."

"Didn't you often wish me dead during our journey up the river?" the colonel asked.

"Perhaps," Cole said. "Yes."

"Then here's your chance. The blade is very sharp."

Cole looked down at the knife. "Colonel, Rebecca would never forgive me."

"You would rather see her dead than be alive but angry at you, is that it?"

Cole pondered that paradox. "I . . ."

"You are weak, Captain Cole. That's why I chose the *West Wind*."

"How's that?"

"If I had been captain of this boat, I would have smashed it on the first snag I could find after the enemy had taken over my boat, regardless of the loss of the boat, or the men in the hold, or even my own life. It would have been the right thing to do, the honorable thing to do. But I knew you wouldn't do it. And look what it's gotten you. Your boat's gone anyway, and dozens of lives have been lost. All you have now is your own miserable life, and that not for long if you don't leave here."

Cole's anger flared. He clenched his teeth and brought the knife blade close to Kingsley's neck.

But his anger faded with a realization that had been gnawing at him for some time, trying to reach his consciousness. The man was right. He, Cole, had chosen the easy way each time, rationalizing, when all along he really knew the proper course of action to take.

"You're right, Colonel," Cole confessed. He lowered the knife.

Kingsley rolled his head to look at Cole. "Well, here is a chance to redeem yourself, Captain. Kill me. Come, I am getting impatient." He rolled his head away again.

"I can't," Cole said. "What if she wouldn't even get in the yawl with me after I had killed you. And I can't ask her for her permission to kill you. She'd refuse it. I just can't do it, Colonel."

"And neither can I," Kingsley said with disgust. "But I am unable to, whereas you are unwilling to. Her life is now on your head, Captain. Please get out of here."

Cole nodded. "Yes, sir."

He backed out of the cabin. If Kingsley had struggled for the knife, Cole thought he probably could have killed him. But to just lie there and let another man cut his throat? Cole shuddered.

He stared down at the knife in his hand. This was the only weapon aboard the *West Wind*. They had no chance when the Sioux boarded. But Rebecca wouldn't leave, and he wouldn't leave Rebecca.

Cole headed for her cabin. Her inside cabin door was open, and he saw her at the outside one, again staring off at the hills. He stepped in, the knife still in his hand.

Rebecca turned. Her eyes fell on the knife, and she looked up at Cole. There was a look of bewilderment on her face.

"This is for you," he said. He tossed the knife onto a small table, then pointed out the door. "You mustn't let the Sioux capture you alive," he warned gently.

She smiled, then reached under her pillow and extracted a shard of broken mirror. "I am way ahead of you, Captain."

Cole nodded. "I should've known."

"What did my father talk to you about?"

"He asked me to kill him with this knife, so that you would leave in the yawl with me."

She sucked in her breath. "And did you kill him?" she asked calmly.

Cole blinked at her coolness. "No."

"Good. I would have killed you in return."

Cole smiled. "That's was the one thing I hadn't thought of," he said.

He sat down in a chair. "I've decided that your father and I have a lot in common," he said.

Rebecca looked at him askance. "I certainly don't see that," she said.

"You can always see other people more clearly than you can see yourself. I always saw your father as a man who just couldn't accept that the Confederacy was dead long ago. So he carried out this so-called mission of his and caused incredible destruction and death. And now he is going to lose his own life as well, probably, as yours.''

She came closer. ''His cause was noble,'' she said testily.

Cole held up a hand. ''But I have done the same thing.''

''You?'' Now her voice softened and she came up even closer.

Cole nodded. ''I couldn't accept losing the *West Wind*. So I did what was needed to keep her afloat. And people died, other boats were lost, and I lost the *West Wind* anyway. And I guess I will lose my own life.''

Cole stared up at Rebecca, though he couldn't see her features very well in the darkness. She stepped very close to him and put out her hands to rest them on his shoulders. ''I am sorry,'' she said. And he knew she really meant it.

She continued. ''Captain Cole, the same applies to me.''

''You mean wanting the war to go on, to avenge your mother's death?''

She nodded. ''So I helped father.'' Her hands slipped from his shoulders. ''But I've done a lot of thinking lately. Ever since the battle with *Big Horn*. About the war, about mother, father, all the dead. And all those wounded who just slipped through my fingers one by one. I've decided that I don't know what's right or wrong anymore. I don't know whose cause was the right cause. What was just and what unjust. Should the war have been fought? Was the war worth all the dying, the misery and destruction?''

''I suspect a lot of people, North and South, feel that it wasn't, Miss Kingsley.''

''So I'm going to start all over. Forget the war, the pain, the deaths, the hurt. Just start all over. Erase, as it were, everything up until now.''

Rebecca made no move, and neither of them said anything for a moment.

''There's another way in which your father and I are alike,'' Cole said. ''Your father was willing to sacrifice his life for a chance to save yours, and I—I guess—''

She suddenly sat down in the chair next to him. "And you chose to stay here instead of getting on the *Mountain Queen*." She put an arm around his neck and rested her head on his shoulder. "Why don't you leave in the yawl by yourself, Captain? Please."

"I'm in love with you, Miss Rebecca Kingsley," Cole said. "I can't leave."

Now she put her other arm around his neck. "And I am in love with you, Captain Zachary Cole." She reached up and kissed him on the cheek. "What do your friends call you, sir?"

"Zach. They call me Zach."

"Well, Zach, my friends call me Beck."

Chapter Eighteen

"Zach," Rebecca whispered.

"Hm?" He jumped when he realized that he had actually fallen asleep in the chair. He sat up straight and looked at Rebecca.

"I thought I heard something," she said, raising her head from his shoulder.

Cole concentrated. All he could hear was the Missouri River slapping against the *West Wind's* superstructure. Then he heard a definite clunk—wood on wood. His scalp cringed.

He stared into the darkness outside the cabin door, listening for the sound to be repeated. It was, followed by wood scraping wood and then the sound of splashing.

"The Sioux have come already, haven't they?" she said.

"Maybe." Cole freed his arm from around her and stood up quickly. He grabbed Kingsley's knife from the table.

Rebecca stood also, clutching at Cole's arm. "I thought Indians didn't like to fight at night."

"Doesn't mean they won't. Besides, they may think the *West Wind's* deserted."

"Somehow I didn't think they would use a boat," Rebecca said.

"May not be a boat," Cole said. "Could be just a log they used to hang onto to get out here." He looked at her. "I won't mislead you, Beck," he said. "There's absolutely no chance that I can fight off a band of Sioux with just a knife."

"I understand."

"I'll fight 'em till I'm dead. That'll give you as much time as possible, but . . . "

She leaned forward and kissed him.

"Beck, I wish I'd—I wish things were different. I wish we were on our way to Fort Benton or back in St. Joseph or . . . "

"Me too," she said softly.

Cole wrapped his arms around her one more time and hugged her tightly. "Goodbye, Beck," he said. "I love you."

She clutched him in return. "Goodbye, Zach. I love you."

Slowly he withdrew his arms and headed for the inside cabin door and peered out. He could see no movement in the salon. He slipped out of the cabin and headed up the line of cabins. He wanted to confront the Indians as far away from Rebecca as possible.

Suddenly a man came out of Kingsley's cabin, and Cole ducked inside another one. He flattened himself against the inside bulkhead and waited for the Indian to approach.

The man was making little noise. Even though he was walking through several inches of water, only an occasional gurgle betrayed his presence.

Cole tensed, waiting for the dim figure to move past his hiding place. When the man's back suddenly appeared in front of the cabin doorway, Cole charged, grabbed the man's throat with his left hand and brought the knife blade swinging around in front with his right hand, aiming for the throat, trying to make one long slice.

But the Indian dropped a rifle into the water and stopped Cole's knife hand with a swift thrust of his own hand, clamping an iron grip on Cole's wrist. The other hand came up in another lightning move. Cole's arm was jerked forward and down, and to Cole's surprise and alarm, he found himself vaulting over the man's back.

He landed in the water, flat on his back. He held tightly to the knife, knowing that if he dropped it, he'd never find it again in the dark.

The Indian's hand shot out and retrieved his rifle from the water. He lunged at Cole, and Cole rolled just as a bayonet drove itself into the carpeted deck.

An Indian using a bayonet? Cole thought.

"Stand still, you savage," the man snarled as he jerked the bayonet out of the planking. He lunged again.

"Devlin!" Cole shouted.

The bayonet stopped halfway toward Cole again. "Cole?"

Cole got to his feet. "What are you doing here, Devlin?"

Devlin grabbed Cole by an arm. "Cole!" He shook him. "It *is* you. I never been so glad to see anybody in my life."

"But what are you doing here?" Cole demanded excitedly.

"I was comin' to see if Miss Rebecca was all right."

"No, no. I mean, what are you doing back on the *West Wind* at all?" Cole clapped the man on the shoulder. "I was going to cut your throat. You should be miles away by now."

Devlin cursed mightily. "We're stuck on a sandbar a couple o' miles upriver," Devlin explained. He rested the butt of his rifle on the deck and clutched the muzzle with both hands.

"Sergeant Devlin?" Rebecca asked.

"Miss Rebecca," Devlin returned happily, seeing her enter the salon from her cabin.

"But what happened?" Cole asked, exasperated.

"Well, first Raasch shot Moore—"

"What?" burst out Cole. "Why?"

"Well, as soon as that first mate of yours figgered out you weren't aboard the *Mountain Queen*, he turned the boat around and headed back downstream. Raasch shot him."

"Is he dead?" Cole asked anxiously.

"No. Bullet tore a chunk out of his left arm, though. But Moore won't cooperate at all anymore. Just sits there and stares at Raasch."

"How'd you get stuck on the sandbar?"

"Raasch! He turned the boat upriver again and ran right into a bar. He tried to get the *Mountain Queen's* engineer to show us how to spar over it, but the man's a blubbering wreck. He keeps moanin' that we're doomed anyway. Says if Raasch doesn't sink us, the Sioux will get us. Keeps whimperin' about how there are rapids ahead that the boat can't get up by herself. He says we have to warp the boat. Says we gotta bury a log ashore."

"That's right, a deadman. Then you use a capstan and a line to the log to pull the boat over the rapids."

Devlin wiped a hand over his mouth. "Well, that engineer has the problem figgered well. We hardly have any men left, compared to the Sioux. We can't send a small party ashore to bury a log; the Sioux would kill the lot of 'em. Just gettin' wood is goin' to be enough of a problem. We could've held 'em off with a field gun and canister but we don't have either."

"How about fishing out the cannon on the *West Wind's* bow?"

"No point to it even if we could. Any powder that wasn't washed away was soaked. But that's beside the point. When the engineer wouldn't help, Raasch tried sparrin' himself, but one of the spars broke."

"Not as easy as it looks, is it, Devlin?" Cole said.

"No, sir, it sure ain't. And not only that, when that spar broke, Raasch let all the tension out of the other ropes, and the other spar dropped and pulled the boat right up over it. We're sittin' on it now."

"Did you try to back off with the wheel?" Cole asked.

"Yeah, but she's stuck tight. And we tried to lighten the boat, too, but the *Mountain Queen* didn't have enough cargo left to make any difference."

"Nobody brings cargo from Fort Benton, Devlin, only to it."

Rebecca spoke. "What really brought you back here, Sergeant?"

"We come back to try to get the spars off the *West Wind*."

"Getting the spars off the *West Wind* and towing them back upstream would be a lot harder than you think," Cole said. "Those spars are heavy."

But Devlin was still looking at Rebecca. "I didn't know if you'd still be here or not. Thought maybe the Sioux might've gotten to you already." His voice trailed off. "Glad to see you're all right, Miss Rebecca."

"Thank you, Sergeant."

"The colonel doesn't seem too good, though. Can't hardly talk."

"He's not doing well."

Devlin nodded slowly.

"Who else is out there?" Cole asked.

"Oh, just Murphy. Raasch and Harris were comin' later. Thomas and Wiley are watchin' on the *Mountain Queen*. Murphy and me were supposed to start gettin' the spars loose." Devlin cupped a hand to his mouth. "Hey, Murphy, come see who's still alive!"

They waited a moment, then heard a man sloshing through the water.

Murphy came up close and looked. "Stars and bars, it's Captain Cole," he exclaimed, chuckling. "Raasch's boat is just about here. Wait till he sees you."

They heard another boat clunk up against the *West Wind*. Raasch, followed by Harris, Wiley, and Thomas, soon entered the salon. Raasch was still carrying Cole's Henry rifle. "You can skip those spars, Devlin," Raasch said. "We're just gonna take the yawls and—" His head jerked forward when he realized that Cole was standing in front of him.

The Henry came up slowly. "So, I'm gonna get the pleasure of killin' you after all."

"Wait a minute, Raasch," Murphy objected. "I got a lot more faith in Cole gettin' us out of this mess than you."

But Raasch just kept raising the Henry. Devlin's rifle barrel came up just as Raasch fired. The bullet went wide and Cole leaped for one of the cabins. Rebecca screamed.

Raasch cursed at Devlin and drove the Henry's butt into Devlin's jaw. The sergeant fell to the deck with a splash. Murphy went to help him up. "Raasch, you're a fool!"

Raasch levered another cartridge into the chamber as he ran toward the cabin Cole had entered. He went all the way through the cabin, looked both ways on the promenade, then jerked his head up. He raised the rifle's muzzle and fired into the hurricane deck overhang.

"I know you're up there, Cole," Raasch yelled. "I can hear you." Again and again he fired bullets into the hurricane deck above.

Devlin and the other four Confederates all crowded through the cabin door. "Don't kill him, Raasch," Devlin shouted. "We need him." He was nursing his jaw.

"No we don't," Raasch said. He was still looking up, trying to guess Cole's location from the sound of his footsteps, but Cole had stopped moving. "I'm goin' up there," he said.

Devlin grabbed his arm. "No you're not." His eyes were glaring. "We need him, Raasch," Devlin warned.

"No, we don't," Raasch said slowly, squinting at Devlin. "I brought the strongbox on that boat, along with plenty of food and ammunition. I was going to have us all head downriver, but I just realized that I don't really need any of you anymore." He was now looking down at Devlin's hand on his sleeve.

Murphy took a wet step forward. "What do you mean, Raasch?"

Raasch drove the butt of the Henry into Murphy's stomach. The corporal had not been expecting the blow, and he crumpled to his knees, gripping his stomach.

Raasch took a step back and brought the barrel up. "All of you, drop your guns."

Harris, Wiley, and Thomas instantly dropped their guns. Devlin tried to snap his up, but Raasch clubbed him on the side of the head with flat of the Henry's stock and Devlin fell face-first into the water.

"No!" Rebecca screamed. She ran to Devlin, dropped to her knees and rolled his face out of the water. "There's been enough killing, Captain Raasch."

"I don't need to kill any of you," Raasch said. "I'm just goin' to take the boat alone, just the gold and me."

"You forgettin' about the Sioux, Raasch?" Murphy asked. He was kneeling on the deck with his hands pressed to his stomach. "Particularly since you're the one they want the most."

Raasch pondered that. "Okay, I'll give 'em something maybe they'll like better than me." He pointed the Henry's rifle at Rebecca. "Get in the boat, Miss Stuck-up."

"Raasch, you can't do that," Murphy said. He got to his feet.

"I won't go with you," Rebecca said.

Raasch said, "I'll drag you into the boat with my bare hands, but I'll have to kill all these men first to do it. Do you go on your own, or do I start shootin'?"

"Don't do it, Miss Rebecca," Murphy said. Harris, Wiley, and Thomas started edging back inside the cabin. Raasch turned swiftly and shot Harris in the stomach and the man slammed against the doorjamb and fell onto the deck with a splash.

Raasch levered another cartridge into the chamber and pointed the gun at Murphy. "Well?" Raasch asked Rebecca. "Should I shoot him, too?"

Murphy's eyes were wide, his heart was pounding, and he took a feeble step backwards. Thomas cowered against the door.

"All right," Rebecca said. "I'll go with you."

"Oh, Miss Rebecca," Murphy moaned. But he didn't ask her not to go.

"Good," Raasch said. He motioned with the rifle barrel. "Toward the front."

Rebecca sloshed through the water to the bow of the *West Wind* with Raasch backing up behind her, keeping the other men covered. He motioned again with the Henry and she climbed reluctantly into one of the yawls, next to the strongbox and sacks of provisions. Raasch untied the other yawl and set it adrift. It quickly disappeared into the darkness. Then he got into the yawl with Rebecca. "Don't try anything," he said. And then he suddenly raised the Henry and cuffed her hard alongside the head.

She nearly fell out of the boat from the blow. With tears in her eyes and a screaming pain in her head she straightened up slowly.

"You move at all and I'll beat you senseless," he growled at her.

Her head was throbbing. She knew she didn't want to get hit again, so she sat very still.

Raasch untied the yawl and pushed away from the *West Wind* with an oar. He sat between the front oarlocks and laid the Henry across his lap. He quickly had both oars in the water, and a few powerful strokes had the yawl away from the sunken steamboat. He shouted toward the *West Wind*. "Don't nobody try to follow me with the *West Wind's* boats," he called. "I'm facin' backwards and I'll see you and pump lead into you. And if you try to shoot me, you'll hit little Miss Stuck-up here."

Raasch saw Murphy, Wiley, and Thomas watching him, motionless on the boiler deck railing. Devlin had gotten up and was checking Harris's still form. Raasch still couldn't see Cole.

He picked up a short length of rope from the bottom of the yawl. "Hold out your hands," he said. She didn't move.

He reached for the Henry, but she quickly raised her hands in front of her.

Raasch finished tying her hands and smiled. "There, little Miss Stuck-up." He grabbed the oars again and began to row. "Now let's have ourselves a nice trip down the river," Raasch said.

Chapter Nineteen

The Missouri River at first light is usually smooth, and the yawl with Raasch and Rebecca in it cut a wedge of ripples as Raasch rowed. He hadn't rowed very hard, but had been content to let the current do most of the work for him.

Raasch saw the Indians on their ponies slowly keeping pace with the yawl and turned the yawl toward the shore. "I'm goin' to see if I can bargain with 'em." The Sioux stopped on the blufftops and turned their ponies to face the river, realizing that Raasch intended to beach the boat.

"Captain Raasch," Rebecca asked. Her voice was tight with fear. "Have you heard what Indians do to white women they capture?"

"If you're nice, they might just make a squaw out of you," Raasch said. But he laughed. He turned to watch the shore as he rowed. "Hey, Indians," he called. "I got somethin' here you might like."

But two hands suddenly leaped out of the water and clamped down on the gunwales by the port oarlock. Rebecca screamed. All Raasch could do was open his mouth in surprise as Cole leaped out of the water and put all of his weight on the side of the yawl, capsizing the boat.

All three people went under and came up sputtering. "I'll kill you, Cole," Raasch screamed.

"Beck, grab the yawl," Cole shouted.

Rebecca's hands were still tied but she threw her arms

177

over the overturned stern and held on with her fingers. The current carried the yawl downstream.

Cole and Raasch found that they could stand. Raasch leaped for Cole, and the two men went under again, but Cole discovered a weakness in Raasch's attack—Raasch was a poor swimmer. Cole had grown up on the river and was an expert swimmer. Whenever Raasch clamped his hands on Cole, Cole simply ducked under and Raasch let go.

Desperately, Raasch drew his pistol, cocking it as he brought it out of the water. He pulled the trigger. The cap snapped, but the pistol didn't fire.

"Your paper cartridges are wet, Raasch," Cole said, leaping for the Confederate.

Raasch threw the useless pistol at Cole and caught the captain on the head. Cole's head spun and he fell over in the water.

Raasch turned and started charging through the water after the yawl. The vessel was not in the main channel, and Raasch was catching up.

When Cole finally got his equilibrium back he saw that Raasch would reach the yawl before he could catch up to him. There was no point in diving for Raasch's pistol, but his Henry had metallic cartridges that would still work. The Henry, though, was somewhere on the bottom of the river.

Cole dove under. They had not moved from the spot where he had overturned the yawl. Opening his eyes didn't do much good, but with his hands he quickly found the strongbox and the provisions. After two more frantic dives, he found the Henry where it had sunk into the ooze. He brought it up triumphantly.

Rebecca screamed Cole's name.

Cole looked for the yawl. Raasch had caught up to it and had yanked Rebecca off and was now dragging her toward the shore.

Cole surged through the water. He made a direct line for the beach; he could travel faster once he was on shore.

Raasch and Rebecca reached the shore first. Raasch headed downstream, still dragging Rebecca. She fought, but Raasch slapped her hard twice and almost rendered her unconscious. After that she was more cooperative.

Cole reached the shore, raised the Henry, and fired a warning shot. The bullet kicked up sand to Raasch's left. He didn't want to risk trying to kill Raasch from this distance; he might hit Rebecca. Cole started to run.

"Let her go, Raasch," Cole yelled.

Raasch, exhausted, stopped and turned. Rebecca slumped to the ground and Raasch threw an arm around Rebecca's waist and yanked her to her feet. He reached around behind and brought out a long sheath knife. Even in the dim light of dawn the blade had a mean glint to it.

Raasch put the edge of the blade to Rebecca's throat. "Back away, Cole. This knife is so sharp, her head will roll if I slice with it," Raasch shouted. Rebecca's eyes were wide with fright. She could feel the sharp steel on her skin.

Cole slid to a stop and raised the Henry, drawing a bead on Raasch's head. It would be a risky shot, but Rebecca was as good as dead if he didn't. He pulled the trigger.

Nothing happened. Angrily Cole worked the lever again, but no empty shell ejected. Raasch had never reloaded the rifle after firing all those shots into the hurricane deck.

Raasch yelped in glee. He threw Rebecca aside and she hit the sand hard and rolled. Raasch gave a Rebel yell and charged, waving his knife over his head. Cole turned the Henry around and grabbed the barrel and swung it hard just as Raasch reached him, but Raasch ducked and lunged and collided with Cole.

Cole was knocked over and Raasch landed on top of him, raising the knife for a swift plunge. But Cole grabbed Raasch's hand with both of his and the two men rolled across the wet sand. Raasch shifted the knife to his other hand, and Cole grabbed both of his wrists. They continued to roll and buck across the ground, trying to toss each other off.

Suddenly the Henry's butt came crashing down and glanced off the side of Raasch's head and hit Cole in the shoulder. Both men looked up to see Rebecca raising the Henry again, her hands still tied but holding the rifle's barrel firmly.

Raasch rolled into Rebecca and she went down with a cry and dropped the Henry. Cole let go of one of Raasch's hands and drove his fist into Raasch's face. Raasch grunted from the impact, but he didn't lessen the pressure of the knife. Cole hit him again and again. Finally Raasch rolled sharply to the other side, breaking free of Cole's grasp.

Cole grabbed the Henry and swung it with one hand as Raasch got to his knees. The rifle hit Raasch's knife hand, and the knife flew away.

Raasch scrambled to his feet, but Cole was right behind him. Raasch dove for the knife, grabbed it and started to roll. Cole landed on top of him.

Raasch screamed once and stiffened. Cole hesitated. Raasch wasn't moving, though his head was up and he was propped on an elbow. Cole looked down and saw that the knife blade had been driven deep into Raasch's chest.

Cole let go slowly and stood up. Raasch didn't move for a few moments, he just stared wide-eyed at the sand. Then his eyelids settled and he slumped to the ground.

Cole was panting hard and his heart was racing. He wiped a hand across his mouth. Rebecca had managed to get to a sitting position, and Cole trotted the few steps to her side and sank to his knees. He cradled her in his arms.

"Zach," she said quietly. "The Sioux are coming."

Chapter Twenty

Cole's head turned. In his fear for Rebecca he had completely forgotten the Indians. Now the Sioux had descended from the bluffs and were pounding their ponies across the sand toward them. There were eight of them. Eight warriors who had fiercely dogged the steamboat's journey for hundreds of miles, thirsty for the blood of revenge. And now there was nothing between them and Cole and Rebecca except a few short yards of open ground.

The Sioux brought their ponies to a sudden stop thirty feet short of the pair. The ponies pranced and kicked up wet sand.

Rebecca squeezed tightly to Cole. "The one in front is one of the chief's sons," she said. "Raasch killed his mother and some of his children."

Cole gripped her more tightly.

The chief's son threw a leg over the head of his pony and jumped to the ground. He was holding an old Springfield carbine. He barely glanced at Cole and Rebecca but strode over to Raasch's body. With an angry shove, he rolled the dead man over with his foot. The Indian studied Raasch's form for a moment. Then he leaned down and yanked the knife from Raasch's chest. He turned and headed for Cole and Rebecca. As he walked he slowly wiped each side of the bloody blade on each of his cheeks.

Cole got quickly to his feet and awkwardly helped Rebecca to hers. He pressed her behind himself and faced the Indian.

The chief's son was tall and solidly built, with huge hands and muscular arms. Cole could plainly see the anger and determination in the warrior's face, and the blood smeared on his cheeks heightened the effect. Cole's jaw tightened and he made ready to spring at the Indian.

The Sioux warrior stopped six feet from Cole. He studied Cole and looked carefully at Rebecca, who peered from behind Cole with eyes wide, her fingernails dug into Cole's arms.

The warrior suddenly flipped the knife in the air and caught it by the flat of the blade. He extended it toward Cole.

Cole was astonished. He slowly reached for the knife and took it from the Indian.

The chief's son tapped himself on the chest and gestured toward the other Sioux on their ponies. Then he slowly pointed downriver. He turned and strode to his pony, leaping onto the pony's back. He yelled to the other Indians and the eight Sioux whirled their ponies and pounded down the shore toward the bluff.

"What are they doing?" Rebecca asked. She still hid behind Cole, but her head was stretched around his shoulder.

Cole straightened up and let out a deep breath. "They're going home," he said.

Chapter Twenty-One

Devlin and Murphy arrived in one of the *West Wind's* yawls shortly after the Sioux left.

"We followed you, Miss Rebecca," Devlin said. "We couldn't get close enough to let Raasch see us, but we wouldn't have let those Sioux get you without a fight."

"Thank you, Sergeant," she said. "And you, too, Corporal."

"I'm so ashamed of myself, Miss Rebecca," Murphy said. "I ain't a coward, but—"

"It's all right."

"How did you get here?" Devlin asked Cole.

"I was already in the water before they left the *West Wind.* He never noticed a head bobbing. When he turned toward shore, I quickly caught up."

"And now the Sioux have left," Devlin said. "But even if warpin' over the rapids wouldn't be a problem anymore, the *Mountain Queen* is still stuck on the mud. Do we walk to Fort Benton?"

Cole shook his head. "We'll take a length of anchor chain and rub it back and forth under the *Mountain Queen's* hull. The current will carry away any sand we stir up. That'll dig a little trough for the boat and we'll be able to back off the bar using the sternwheel. Then we go back to the *West Wind* and pick up her spars using the *Mountain Queen's* derricks."

Murphy brightened. "Never thought I'd be so grateful to a Yankee."

Devlin smiled. "Wiley and Thomas will be happy to hear it, too."

"Say," Murphy asked, looking toward the river, "where's the boat Raasch was in?"

"It's headed for St. Louis, upside down," Rebecca said.

"And the strongbox?" Murphy asked. His brow was knit.

Cole nodded toward the river. "Somewhere out there."

"Think we can find it?" Devlin asked.

Cole shook his head slowly. "Only by the greatest luck. I couldn't tell you where the yawl tipped over. And if you don't find it right away, the current will soon have it buried under silt forever."

Murphy sighed audibly.

Devlin shrugged. "Guess it wasn't meant to be." He turned to Cole. "Before we head upriver, Captain, I want to bury Raasch. I know he done wrong, but he fought hard for the Confederacy and for the boys and me. He deserves respect for that."

Cole nodded. "I guess that's proper, Sergeant."

Devlin looked at Rebecca. "And we talked to your father, Miss Rebecca. I don't know if he'll make it or not, but Murphy and Wiley and Thomas and me promised the colonel that we'd carry him to Canada and either bury him there if he dies or see that you and him are set up."

"That's a long march, Devlin," Cole said.

"We owe him," Devlin said.

Murphy nodded vigorous agreement. "We surely do."

"Well, I'll help you, too," Cole said.

"Why, that's right generous of you, Captain Cole," Devlin said. "But I'm surprised."

"Thank you, Zach," Rebecca said. She gave his arm a squeeze.

Devlin thought maybe he understood a little.

"And then home for you men?" Cole asked.

Devlin nodded vigorously. "Home. And I think you'll

like Canada, Miss Rebecca,'' Devlin said. ''Even if the colonel doesn't make it.''

''My father is tough, Sergeant Devlin,'' she said. ''He'll live. And he will like Canada. But I'm coming back to the river.''

Devlin frowned at her. ''The river?'' He saw Rebecca smile up at Cole, and he looked at Cole. He saw the sparkle in the steamboat captain's eyes, and then he chuckled. ''Well, the two of you have been at war most of this trip. I guess if you can make a union, maybe the South and the North can again, too.''

They all laughed.

''Captain,'' Devlin said. ''I thought steamboat men didn't like to walk at all, much less the sixty miles it is from the river to the Canadian border. And then all the way back.''

Cole looked at Rebecca and she smiled at him. He gave her a squeeze. ''It'll be worth it,'' he said.